I want to see

Sophie expelled a ████████ one of relief. "So you're not finding it hard to be around me?" she asked.

Sawyer had to repeat that to himself. "Hard?" he asked.

"Yes," she said. "If I were any other woman, you could kiss me now and not worry about whether I'd scream or tremble or push you away."

Her candor made him grin. "Actually, I get a lot of that anyway."

She elbowed him in the arm. He loved the way she did that. "You do not. I hear that women love you. So do children."

He pushed at the car door, thinking he couldn't take too much more of this. She was studying him with a sweet look that was still mildly wary, for all her speculation on how she'd react if he kissed her.

"I have to go," he said quickly. He got out of her car and walked around to his, only to find her standing in front of his door.

Her mind was replaying bright images of Sawyer holding her in the office, memories of how it felt when a man's muscles were used to comfort rather than hurt.

"Sophie…" he warned.

Dear Reader,

When I began this book I thought I didn't understand daredevils, but I created one in Sawyer Abbott anyway because I know readers love them. Life is such a gift that it seems criminal to me to risk it for anything less than saving another life.

And then it occurred to me that's what we do when we love each other. We save each other. Love is the biggest risk a man or woman can take, and there's no fire suit, no safety net, no 911 responder to protect you from disaster. Love is an openhearted, pull-out-all-the-stops gamble that whatever draws you to someone will grow into the stuff that lasts a lifetime.

As all writers do, I shape a character and send him or her in a certain direction, but what he or she decides to do is really up to that character. When Sawyer decided to love Sophie despite a dark secret, and to love her three creative children, I realized I knew him pretty well. And I fell in love with him myself. I hope you will, too.

Sincerely,

Muriel Jensen

P.O. Box 1168
Astoria, Oregon 97103

Books by Muriel Jensen

HARLEQUIN AMERICAN ROMANCE

866—FATHER FOUND
882—DADDY TO BE DETERMINED
953—JACKPOT BABY*
965—THAT SUMMER IN MAINE
1020—HIS BABY**

*Millionaire, Montana
**The Abbotts

HIS WIFE
Muriel Jensen

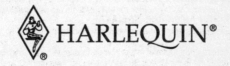

HARLEQUIN®

TORONTO • NEW YORK • LONDON
AMSTERDAM • PARIS • SYDNEY • HAMBURG
STOCKHOLM • ATHENS • TOKYO • MILAN • MADRID
PRAGUE • WARSAW • BUDAPEST • AUCKLAND

ISBN 0-373-75034-X

HIS WIFE

www.eHarlequin.com

Printed in U.S.A.

THE ABBOTTS—A GENEALOGY

Thomas and Abigail Abbott: arrived on the *Mayflower*; raised sheep outside Plymouth

William and Deborah Abbott: built a woolen mill in the early nineteenth century

Jacob and Beatrice Abbott: ran the mill and fell behind the competition when they failed to modernize

James and Eliza Abbott: Jacob's eldest son and grandfather of Killian, Sawyer and Campbell Abbott; married a cotton heiress from Virginia

Nathan Abbott and Susannah Stewart Abbott: parents of Killian and Sawyer; Nathan diversified to boost the business and married Susannah, the daughter of a Texas oilman who owned Bluebonnet Knoll

Nathan Abbott and Chloe Marceau: parents of Campbell and Abigail; renamed Bluebonnet Knoll and made it Shepherd's Knoll

Killian Abbott: now the CEO of Abbott Mills; married to **Cordelia Magnolia Hyatt**

Sawyer Abbott: Killian's brother by blood; a daredevil

Campbell Abbott: half brother to Killian and Sawyer; brother to Abigail; manages the Abbott estate on Long Island

China Grant: thinks she might be the missing Abigail

Sophie Foster: mother of Gracie, Eddie and Emma Foster; the woman with whom Sawyer Abbott falls in love

Brian Girard: half brother to Killian and Sawyer

Prologue

Sawyer Abbott stared into the eyes of the beautiful young woman he'd found peering in the French doors to the library of his home, as he struggled to process what she'd just told him. "I think…" she'd said, "I mean…I believe I could be…your sister, Abigail."

Sister. For so long the word had signified grief and regret and terrible guilt. But connecting any of those to this vibrant young woman with long dark hair and lively dark eyes was difficult. Although those physical characteristics would qualify her.

"I wasn't snooping, I swear," she went on hastily. "I was just hoping for a glimpse of one of you, some sign of a friendly face so that this wouldn't be so… scary."

He wanted to reply, but shock held back the words.

"I'm…China Grant, by the way. I mean…that's been my name. But…maybe not who I really am."

She shifted her weight and smiled a little nervously, pointing to a square box on the ground. It was the utilitarian kind, intended to hold office documents or personal papers for storage. "I, ah…there are some things in my box," she said rapidly, "that make me think it could be me. I was adopted as a toddler and I always knew that, but I was told I came to my family through my mother's doctor. They adopted my sister the same way. When our father died just a month ago, we were cleaning out the house and found these boxes with our names on them, and the things that must have belonged to us when we moved in. I know that probably sounds suspicious…''

She kept talking, and he finally raised a hand to stop her. She sighed, as though grateful. ''Sorry,'' she went on. ''There's just so much to say.''

His brain a muddle of confusion, his emotions taking him places he wasn't sure he had the courage to explore, he nodded in agreement. If she was Abby, there was twenty-five years' worth of things to say.

He pushed the French doors open. ''Let's go inside. Our company's yearly staff meeting is under way here right now, but this room's pretty quiet.''

She walked in, holding on to her box, and stopped in the middle of the room. ''My goodness,'' she whispered. He was used to the room, but the dark wood and leather and floor-to-ceiling shelves of books did have an awesome elegance.

He pointed her to the leather sofa and noticed a mild tremor in his hand. That tremor was beginning to take over his body.

''Wait right here,'' he said. ''I'll get my brothers.''

She put the box down on the coffee table and asked hopefully, ''Is my mother at home?'' Then she added with a little apologetic inclination of her head, ''I mean, if she is my mother.''

Her mother. That possibility was mind-bending after all these years. Chloe would be beside herself with shock and excitement. It was probably a good thing she wasn't here until they could conclude whether or not this woman was Abby.

"She's in Paris at the moment," Sawyer replied. "Her aunt is very ill and she's caring for her."

"I see." Clearly disappointed, she sat.

"Can I get you something?" he asked, touched by her quiet grace. "Coffee? Soft drink?"

"No, thank you." She wore a white sweater and joined her hands on the knees of her white slacks. "I don't think I could swallow. I'll just sit right here and wait for you."

Sawyer hurried down the hallway and through the quiet kitchen. Catering staff were handling this last day of the meeting. Through the window he could see them setting up under one of several pavilions on the lawn.

His breath came quickly as he ran upstairs, the expansion of his lungs making his broken ribs hurt. Imagining now that his near-fatal waterskiing accident had occurred less than twenty-four hours ago was hard. He should slow down, but he couldn't. Abigail was home—maybe.

He rapped on his elder brother's bedroom door. Killian opened it, a shushing finger to his lips. "Cordie's still asleep." He pulled on a blue cotton sweater, then took a good look into Sawyer's eyes. Killian's were blue under dark blond hair slightly disheveled by the sweater. "What?" he asked anxiously.

Sawyer pointed downstairs. "There's a young woman in the library." He was breathless.

"Yeah?"

"She says she thinks she's Abby."

"What?" Killian demanded.

Sawyer told him about the box.

"What's in it?"

"I don't know. I thought the three of us should talk to her together."

Killian went into CEO mode. He lived his life with the same methodical organization he used to lead the Abbott Mills Corporation. Sawyer headed up the family's charitable foundation, and Campbell, their younger brother, managed the estate. "Is Campbell downstairs?" Killian tugged his sweater into place over stone-colored slacks.

"He was still sleeping when I left the boathouse." Sawyer and his younger brother had slept there because of the crowd at the house. "I'm going for him right now."

"Okay. I'll meet you in the library in ten minutes."

Sawyer rushed down the stairs and toward the back door, a hand to his screaming ribs. He was halfway across the back lawn when Campbell appeared on the trail, walking toward the house in jeans and a black Abbott Mills T-shirt. He ran a hand through his dark hair, yawning.

"Hi," he said when he spotted Sawyer. "I heard you get up and leave, and thought that meant you were coming back with doughnuts. Where are—?" He stopped when his dark eyes settled on Sawyer's face. "What happened?" he asked urgently.

"We have a visitor," Sawyer replied, taking Campbell's arm and hurrying him toward the house, "who thinks she's Abby."

Campbell froze in the middle of the trail, though the late-June Long Island morning was already growing warm. "What? What makes you think she's telling the truth?"

"I have no idea if she is or not," Sawyer admitted, drawing him forcefully along. "I just thought we should all talk to her. I left her in the library and Killian's going to meet us there."

"All right, all right. I'm coming." Campbell yanked free of him. "She's probably pocketing our first editions as we speak. Why on earth would Abby just show up after all this time? She's got to be some larcenous babe after part of the Abbott fortune."

Somehow, Sawyer didn't think so. "Don't make judgments before you meet her."

"And don't start calling her 'sis' before we know the truth."

Killian was filling the coffeemaker when Sawyer and Campbell arrived. A long granite-topped counter served as a work area for Killian, who used the library as an office. In a corner was a small wet bar and a coffeepot.

"Ah. Here they are." Killian pulled cups out from under the counter as China Grant stood uncertainly at their arrival. Killian had apparently already introduced himself, and Sawyer could only guess from the hospitable act of coffee-making that his brother had decided she was worth listening to.

Sawyer introduced Campbell. "He's the youngest brother. Killian and I are Abigail's half brothers, from our father's first wife, but Campbell is her full sibling. Still, we're all very close and none of us notices that we aren't all full-blooded relations." He sent Campbell a look that told him to keep his personal confusion about his place in the family to himself.

She offered her hand. "Hello," she said in a warm, quiet voice. "I'm China Grant. That is, that's who I've been for twenty-five years. I'm not sure who I was for the fourteen months before that."

Campbell shook her hand politely, but didn't bother to hide his skepticism. "What makes you think you're our sister?"

"I found these things...." She pointed to the box she'd carried in. The name China was printed on the lid in broad-tipped black pen. "I did a little research about your family and thought...I might be related."

"Why?"

Killian encouraged China to sit on the sofa and took the other end of it. Sawyer saw him send Campbell a look that told him to show a little courtesy.

Campbell held his stare without flinching as he sat in a chair opposite the sofa. Sawyer sat in the matching chair.

China removed the lid from the box, pulled out several yellowed newspaper clippings and handed them to Killian. She folded her hands as she watched him scan them.

"They're all stories of your sister's kidnapping," she said. "I can't imagine why my parents would have saved them in my box if they didn't relate to me."

Killian's expression grew grim as he passed one clipping to Sawyer and perused another.

"Then," China went on, pulling a pair of light blue corduroy rompers out of the box, "there're these." She exposed the label sewn into the back of them. It was the same label Abbott Mills's children's wear division used today. Abbott Mills Baby, with a lamb curled atop the double *L*. In the logo for the company's other products, a sheep stood on the double *L*.

"We sold millions of those," Campbell challenged. "Anybody could…"

But Sawyer had a nebulous memory of a favorite pair of rompers the nanny always put on Abby because of their durability and the baby's high-speed crawl. The knees were reinforced with star-shaped patches.

China held the garment up by the straps, the patches worn, two corners of one star unraveled.

Sawyer's heart slammed against his aching ribs.

Killian took the rompers from her and studied them, frowning with concentration.

"I remember them," Sawyer said softly.

Killian nodded. "I think I do, too." He ran a hand over the knee patches. "She used to crawl everywhere," he said, lost in his thoughts. "None of our stuff was safe from her." He passed the garment to Sawyer.

"I repeat," Campbell said firmly, "that Abbott Mills made thousands of grosses of those."

"I'll bet," China said, lifting something else out of the box, "that there aren't thousands of grosses of these." She drew out a rag doll wearing a miniature pair of the same rompers, with the same star patches. The doll had obviously been specially made, with style and skill. It had painted eyes, cheeks and lips, and elegantly embroidered eyelashes. Brown yarn hair was woven into long braids.

"I think…Chloe made this," Killian whispered. "Abby carried it with her all the time."

Campbell crossed the room to take the doll from

him. "How can you be so certain this is the same doll? It was twenty-five years ago."

"I'm not certain," Killian said. He looked startled, even a little shaken. "But I think there's enough here that bears investigating."

"Okay," Campbell said. "All we need for proof is a DNA test."

Killian put a hand to his forehead. "Yeah, but Mom's worried about Tante Bijou at the moment, and I hate to further upset her with the news that a woman who might be her daughter has come to Shepherd's Knoll. She won't want to leave Tante Bijou, but she'll be frantic— Her aunt raised her," he explained to China, "and she's in very poor health. Mom's very worried about her."

"Then don't tell her," China said in a reasonable tone, packing up her box again. "Wait until she comes home. The last thing I want to do is cause her pain. I'll leave you my address and phone number in L.A.—"

"No, wait." Killian stood, looking pensive. He went to the counter to pour coffee. "Let's think this through."

"Couldn't we just do the test with me?" Campbell asked. "If she is my full sibling—"

"No." Sawyer didn't like that idea. "Mom should be here before we do anything. She was here when Abby was lost, and she should be in on finding her. If she is Abby."

"And if she isn't?" Campbell demanded impatiently. "Mom gets to grieve all over again? Let's just do it. Then we'll know and we'll spare Mom the pain if she's lying."

"I'm not lying!" China denied with a glower at Campbell. Then her expression softened as she looked to Killian and Sawyer. "I may be wrong about who I am, but I'm not lying. I'm sorry this is hard on all of you. I don't mean it to be. I just don't know how else to learn the truth." She handed Killian a business card and stood.

Taught Chloe's European manners very young, all the brothers stood with her.

"You should stay," Killian said. "We happen to have a houseful at the moment, but they'll all be gone tomorrow. We'll find someplace to put you tonight."

"Killian!" Campbell said in complete exasperation. "What are you talking about? You don't know any—"

"It'll be good for her to stay," Killian repeated. "You'll get to know each other."

"I don't have time to get to know anybody. I have too much to do already."

"I'd be happy to earn my keep," China put in quietly.

"There you go, Cam!" Killian was warming to the whole idea. "You're always telling me that you could use staff to manage the estate. China can help you while she's here."

"But—"

"I think it's a great idea, too," Sawyer put in.

Campbell groaned, predictably exasperated.

"Are you able to stay?" Killian asked her. He glanced at her business card, then up at her. "You own a shopping service in L.A.?"

"Yes." Her quiet manner evaporated in her growing excitement. "I have four great employees. I told them I'd be away a couple of weeks."

Campbell, accustomed to being outvoted on most things since childhood, twirled his index finger in a mockery of delight. "She's good at shopping. That'll help me a lot."

"Do you want to stay?" Sawyer asked her.

She looked right into Campbell's face and answered sweetly, "I'd love to stay. And shopping is an art, smarty. One should be willing to pay a fair price, but never too much."

That, Sawyer thought, sounded a lot like his father.

Killian grinned at him. "That's settled. They'll be working together until Mom comes home. Did I mention Cordie and I are leaving for Italy on our second honeymoon day after tomorrow? You're in charge."

Sawyer closed his eyes, his head now hurting as well as his ribs. If he was going to have to assume Killian's role as an arbitrator while he was gone, it was a good thing he was used to flirting with danger.

Chapter One

Anchovies, pepper jack cheese, wheat crackers, beef jerky, marinated vegetables, oranges and taco-flavored corn chips. Sawyer Abbott checked the list in his hand against the contents of his cart and decided, as he crossed off the last item, that shopping wasn't so hard. Kezia Chambers, the Abbott family's housekeeper at Shepherd's Knoll, had laughed when he'd told her he was headed for the Losthampton Market.

"You're going to meet girls, aren't you?" She was African-American and she and her husband, Daniel, the Abbotts' chauffeur, had been part of the family for as long as Sawyer could remember. Over the years, she'd alternately scolded him and comforted him and his brother Killian, depending upon the situation. When their mother had left he was three and Killian was five, and she'd helped them accept their stepmother, Chloe, and the two babies she and their father had eventually added to their household. And when their little sister, Abigail, was taken at fourteen months of age, Kezia had been a brick.

"No, I'm not." He'd pretended to be insulted. "As

if I *had* to arrange to meet single women. They seem to find me.''

She'd rolled her eyes as she stirred the dark contents of a bowl with a wooden spoon. "You're *so* spoiled. You were born with those fair good looks and that outrageous charm and you think they'll never fail you, but someday you're going to meet someone who'll resist you. Then what will you do?"

"Nothing," he replied. "I won't want anyone who doesn't want me. Now—do you need anything from the market? I just came to ask you as a courtesy. Don't try to harass me the way you harass Killian."

"Really?" She smiled and raised the wooden spoon from the bowl menacingly. A rich chocolate batter ran off the spoon, its sweet aroma wafting toward him. Brownies. "Even if I'm making your favorite treat?"

"Are you putting caramel and pecans in them?" he bargained.

"I might be convinced to do that, but you have to let me pick on you."

He'd rolled his eyes theatrically. "Oh, all right. But there'd better be lots of caramel."

"There will be. If you'd remember to give me your list when I go shopping, you wouldn't have to pick up your own treats. China's been here only two weeks and *she* remembers to tell me what she needs."

"I know. She's obviously smarter than I am. I'm just laying in a few personal supplies. Brian and I are working on one of his boats tonight, and even though he has that little store now, he has mostly survival stuff for tourists and none of my favorites."

"Ha!" she teased. "Applaud him for his good taste."

Brian Girard, a newly discovered half brother, the progeny of Sawyer and Killian's perfidious mother and the next-door neighbor, had upped the Abbott-sibling count to five. Sawyer, Killian and Campbell— their other half brother and full sibling of Abigail— had been doing their best to make him feel welcome. Brian had refused Killian's invitation to move into Shepherd's Knoll, choosing instead to live in an old house his paternal grandmother had left him. He'd recently bought an old general store and boat rental at the edge of Losthampton on Long Island, and was learning about life as a merchant after having spent most of his adulthood in the corporate world with Corbin Girard, his natural father.

The fact that Corbin had hated and competed with the Abbotts and the Abbott Mills Corporation all his life was ignored by the brothers as they determined to make their own way in this new relationship.

And since Brian had literally saved Sawyer's life when one of Sawyer's stunts for charity had gone wrong, Sawyer felt obliged to make even more of an effort than the others. Actually, Brian was hardworking and witty, and liking him didn't require much effort. His father had disowned him for helping the Abbotts, and without the old man's predatory presence among them, they were getting along very well.

Sawyer suddenly remembered something he'd forgotten to put on the list but had thought about on the drive to town—the current *Wall Street Journal*. He'd promised Killian he'd keep an eye on their stock while he was gone.

Sawyer pushed his cart through the narrow aisles
of the quaint little store that hadn't changed much in
one hundred and fifty years because its nineteenth-
century-charm appealed to the tourists. He stopped at
the book and magazine rack in back. Someone had
apparently just rummaged through the newspapers on
the bottom, so the usually orderly stacks were all jum-
bled. Sawyer squatted behind the rack to look for the
Journal.

"Mister!" A high, urgent whisper made him look
up into the dark eyes of a boy about eight. He was
scrawny and flushed and appeared frightened. With
him was a little girl slightly younger, who had the
same dark eyes and tumbled dark hair. She, too,
looked scared. Their hands and faces were dirty.

"What is it?" Sawyer asked, putting a hand to the
boy's shoulder.

"Can you help us?" the boy asked, his big eyes
pleading.

Sawyer noted the boy's anxious glance around the
book rack.

"With what? What's the matter?"

"We've been kidnapped!" the boy said, ducking.
"We need you to help us!"

Sawyer stared at him. "What? Kidnapped by
whom?"

The little girl nodded and pointed around the rack
to a woman pushing a cart through the produce section. The woman wore a white shirt and denim pedal
pushers and her dark hair was caught in a ponytail.
She stopped to thump a watermelon.

Sawyer stepped back behind the rack and turned to

the little girl, whose lip was trembling. "She took us from our mom in Florida!" she said.

"When?" he asked. That was an irrelevant question under the circumstances, he realized, but he was having trouble believing this was happening to him.

"Three days ago," the boy replied. "We haven't had much to eat. And she hid us in the back of the car under a blanket all the way from Florida."

Sawyer peered out again and saw that the woman, though quite pretty, did seem drawn and tired, as though she had been driving for days. Suddenly, she looked up and around her, and the impatience and annoyance on her face were clear. "Eddie!" she called. "Emma!"

Sawyer leaned out of sight again, took the cell phone out of his pocket and dialed 911. A glance around the rack while he waited for a response told him the woman was headed this way. He caught the little girl by the hand and gestured for the boy to follow.

Emergency picked up and Sawyer explained the situation as he hustled the children across the market to the deli. He put the children behind the meat case and planted himself in the narrow opening between it and a case filled with salads while he finished his call. He told the dispatcher where they were, gave her a physical description of the woman, and rattled off his name and cell phone number. She promised officers would be there within minutes.

He turned off his phone and pocketed it, hearing the woman calling the children. She sounded as though she was going up one aisle and down the other. By the time she reached the deli, she was look-

ing pretty desperate. He wasn't surprised. She was
being deprived of potential ransom money or the fulfillment of some sick need to mother children, *anyone's* children.

Kidnap was not just an ugly headline to him but a
stark reality, an event that had changed his life forever, and he hated to think of another family enduring
such a horrible thing. Well, at least this time the children would be returned and the family wouldn't be
left to wonder for their entire lifetimes if the child
was alive or dead, if she was suffering or terrified.

"Hey!" the boy asked softly from behind the case.
"You're that guy that does the stunts, aren't ya?"

Sawyer nodded and put a finger to his lips.

"Have you got kids?" the little girl whispered
loudly.

As Sawyer turned to quiet her, he heard the boy
answer, "Of course he doesn't, stupid! He isn't even
married!"

"Mom's not married and she's got us!" the girl
replied in a "so there!" tone.

"Shh!" Sawyer hushed them as he saw the woman
come down the aisle, still calling their names.

He felt belligerent as the woman pointed her cart
toward him. To tell her what he thought of her would
have been satisfying, but that might make her run
before the police arrived. And he wanted her put behind bars before she did this to someone else's children.

"Excuse me," the woman said courteously, apologetically. "Have you seen two little children—a boy
and a girl, around this height?" She held a hand, palm

down, about waist high, then a little higher. "Big dark eyes, lots of hair, look a lot like me?"

He was silently applauding her performance as the worried mother when he noticed that the children did look a lot like her. Her eyes were also large and dark, and though her hair was more auburn than brown, it was thick like theirs. The boy had a dimple in his right cheek and so did she.

A horrible possibility began to form in his mind.

But natural mothers were always stealing their children from court-appointed guardians, he reminded himself. Still, the children would know she was their mother. Or would they?

"I don't understand it," she said anxiously. Mild concern was turning to serious fear. "It isn't like them to—"

Before she could finish that sentence, Sawyer saw two policemen coming down the aisle, and he beckoned to them.

She hesitated, turning to see whom he was signaling. Her eyes widened at the sight of the policemen, then she turned back to him in confused surprise. A small crowd had gathered at the head of the aisle to see what the police were up to.

Sawyer recognized one of the officers as David Draper. He was tall, craggy-faced and middle-aged, a seasoned veteran of the force. He and Sawyer had worked together on community fund-raising.

Draper stopped halfway down the aisle. The younger officer, a stranger to Sawyer, also stopped, clearly wondering what Draper was doing. Draper shook his head then kept coming.

"This your kidnapper?" Draper asked Sawyer, one

hand on his leather belt, the other on the butt of his holstered gun. He aimed his chin at the woman.

Sawyer nodded. "She took the kids three days ago from someplace in Florida. They haven't had anything to eat and she's kept them under a blanket in the back of her car."

The woman expelled a gasp of dismay and put both hands to her face.

Aha! Sawyer thought, vindicated by that expression of guilt. *Gotcha!*

"She's a hard case, all right," Draper said. "Goes by the name Sophie Foster. ER nurse at Losthampton Hospital, sings at St. Paul's Catholic Church—eight-thirty mass—and helps out at the crisis shelter for battered women. But she does have a problem with kids."

"Stealing them?" Sawyer asked, not sure what to make of Draper's description.

"No, raising them," Draper replied. "She appears to have two little frauds on her hands. Can I see the children in question?"

This was not looking good. Sawyer could feel himself physically shrinking. He was about two feet high now. He reached behind the case and pulled out the boy. Inexplicably, the boy was grinning.

"I found him, Mom!" he exclaimed. "This is him! Brave! Willing to help! Not married! He's perfect!"

The woman dropped her hands with a groan and said to Sawyer in a remarkably even voice, all things considered, "You know what, Mr—?"

"Abbott," Draper provided before Sawyer could.

She was distracted for a moment. "The Shepherd's Knoll Abbotts?" she asked Draper.

He nodded. "Second son."

"Ah." She nodded, then diverted her attention at Sawyer. He waited for the slow perusal women usually gave him that resulted in a smile of admiration, even when they pretended not to be interested. Of course, he'd just called the police on her, so he wasn't entirely surprised when she did nothing but look into his eyes, her own very weary. "Tell you what, Mr. Abbott number two. You obviously care for these children, so how about if I just let you have them? Right now. No charge." She turned to Draper. "That's not a problem for you, is it? I mean, I'm not selling them—I'm just letting him have them."

Eddie grinned up at Sawyer. "She's just kidding. She loves us a lot."

"Of course I do, Eddie" she said to the boy, "but you couldn't possibly love me if you'd do something as mean as make me believe you'd gotten lost. And something as mean to this man as telling him that I'd kidnapped you."

The little girl ran out from behind the case to wrap her arms around her mother's hips. "We did it to help you find a daddy," she said, "not to be mean. 'Cause you just can't find one by yourself."

SOPHIE WOULD HAVE HAPPILY abandoned her children, her job, her little cottage on the water and every one of her meager possessions for life somewhere on the Riviera.

According to novels and movies, life there would involve political intrigues, amassing of jewels or cash, achieving a high social position. Definitely easier than raising three children by herself while trying to erase painful memories and live in a world that seemed to work for everyone else but not for her.

Being trapped in an abusive relationship for several years had left her unable to bear a man's touch, yet with a desperate need for it. She didn't understand it and neither did her psychotherapist. And Father O'Neil could tell her only to keep praying, keep living her life and trusting in God to find her a solution.

She'd been doing that for two years, but there was no light on the horizon that she could see. Added to her confusion was the fact that her two younger children wanted a father so much. They hadn't witnessed as much of Bill's temper as had ten-year-old Gracie, who, like Sophie, didn't want another man in her life. She was withdrawn and skittish, and Sophie ached every time she saw Gracie take a step back when a man approached.

Two of the children wanted a father, and one of them didn't. They manifested, Sophie thought, the dichotomy that existed within herself.

So she prayed, and lived her life, and waited for a solution. Eddie and Emma's current prank was making escape look better and better.

She was mildly entertained, though, by Abbott number two's horrified expression.

"I'm so sorry," he was saying, as Draper talked on his radio. "But they were dirty and seemed so frightened. And I saw you and thought you seemed..." He hesitated over the words on the tip of his tongue. She was enjoying his discomfort just a little; only fair, considering what he was putting her through.

"Cruel?" she asked. "Psychopathic?"

He shook his head guiltily. "No. No. Tired. A little stressed." He put a gentle hand to Eddie's head and smiled wryly. "Now I understand why. I haven't been around kids very much. It didn't occur to me that they'd lie about such a thing."

She was inclined to believe him. "Kids this age are always dirty, and there's a vast uncharted territory in their little minds between truth and fantasy. I just hauled them out of the backyard to go shopping. I should have bathed them first, but I was pressed for time."

Actually, the man was very handsome in a wild Long Island–playboy sort of way. He had dark blond hair, which he wore in a spiked and disheveled style that made him appear youthful and somehow useless. But added to that was a pair of blue eyes that were sharply intelligent and surprisingly gentle at the same time. They were set in a handsome, nicely shaped face that managed to look strong without sharp angles or a square jaw.

He was tall and athletic in simple cotton slacks and a dark blue shirt. She glanced at the contents of his cart. He did have strange taste in food, however.

She didn't want to have to explain to him about her younger children and their obsession about finding a father, but they had used and embarrassed him, and she owed him that much.

"They want a father," she said with a sigh, "and I have no use for another husband, so it's hard for us to come together on a solution to the problem. I just didn't realize they were desperate enough to go searching one out on their own."

"Another husband," he said. "You mean you've already got one?"

She shook her head. "I had one. He's gone."

"He's gone to heaven!" Emma said loudly, the way she said everything.

Sophie wasn't sure that was where he was, but she didn't mind that Emma thought so. That was about all this stranger should know about her difficult past, but she couldn't just walk away until Dave Draper decided what he was going to do about Eddie and Emma.

"I saw your picture in the paper," Eddie said to Sawyer Abbott, looking pleased with himself. "You did that dangerous stunt with the skis and the barrels. And you give lots of money to help children. That's why we picked you out when we saw you buying oranges."

Abbott squatted in front of him. "I'm flattered that you picked me out. But that was a pretty awful thing to do to your mom. What if a policeman had come who didn't know that she really was your mom and he took her off to jail because he really thought she'd kidnapped you?"

The expression on Eddie's face said he'd never considered that.

"I wondered if you'd help us," Eddie said with a frown. "And not just with something easy, but with something really hard. 'Cause a lot of dads don't help with the hard stuff. So, if we're going to find another one, he's got to be great."

Clearly, Sawyer Abbott had no experience with children. Eddie already had him wrapped around his little finger. When Emma put her arm around his neck, he turned to look into her face and Sophie saw his eyes melt.

"Okay, that's it," she said, taking each child by the hand and drawing them back from him. "We'll probably have to go to the police station, but Mr. Abbott didn't do anything wrong, so Officer Draper will just let him go home. I'm sure he's eager to get on his—"

"You have to come with me," Draper announced, tucking away his radio. "Sorry, Mr. Abbott, but the chief wants to see you, too."

"But all he did—" Sophie began to protest.

Draper cut her off with a nod. "I know, I know, but we need a full report," he said with a significant glance at the children, intending to help them realize the gravity of what they'd done. "And in order to do that, we have to have Mr. Abbott's input."

"I'm sorry," she said with a sigh. She'd had a long day at the hospital, and the quick dinner she had planned, followed by a long period with her feet up, didn't look as though it was going to materialize.

Abbott smiled. He had to be the most even-tempered man. "Not a problem. I'll meet you at the station," he said to Draper, who nodded, then took each of her children by the hand and led them toward a roped-off checkout line. The young officer went ahead of him to unhook it, then closed it after him when he followed her and the children through.

People were watching them with frowns, wondering, she was sure, what crime they'd committed. She'd be horrified if she wasn't accustomed to policemen being called, usually on her behalf, and the shocked expressions of neighbors. This wasn't what she wanted for her children. She and the kids would have to have a serious talk about this father-finding stuff when this was over.

She could only hope that being marched out by a police officer was having the desired effect on the children.

That hope was dashed when Eddie looked at her over his shoulder and said with a big grin, "Isn't he great, Mom? He didn't even get mad!"

Chapter Two

"You're going where?" Brian asked, as Sawyer called him on his cell phone.

"The police station," Sawyer repeated a second time. "It's kind of a long story."

"What did you do?"

"Nothing. These kids told me they'd been kidnapped and I called the police on the woman they were with. Turns out she really is their mother."

There was silence on the other end of the line.

"Brian?" Sawyer prompted.

"I'm here," he replied. "I just don't know what to say to that. Are you in trouble, or is she?"

"I think the officer's just making a point, bringing us all in to make an impression on the kids so they don't do it again."

"Why'd they do it in the first place?"

"They're looking for a father."

Sawyer heard stifled laughter. "And they picked *you?*" Brian asked.

"Yes, they did, thank you very much. Seems they read about me in the paper."

"I didn't know kids read the paper."

"Yeah, well, there's apparently a lot you don't know. So, I'll be over later than I'd planned, okay?"

"Sure. Call me if you need bail."

"Ha, ha."

Sawyer pulled into the parking lot of the small police station, with its turn-of-the-century, ball-shaped lights in front of the building. He was right behind Sophie Foster as she climbed the few steps into the building, following the police officers and her children. Sawyer caught up to take her elbow. She had to be feeling terrible.

He was surprised when she recoiled, yanking her arm out of his reach. "Don't!" she said, fear visible in her eyes and the sharp line of her mouth.

He dropped his hand immediately. He'd never frightened anyone that he could recall, except maybe those who'd misused Abbott Mills Foundation funds.

"I'm sorry," he said quickly. "I didn't mean to sneak up on you."

The fear left her expression as she exhaled. "That's all right," she replied, apology in her tone. "I'm just not very…physical."

He nodded. "I was trying to do the gentlemanly thing by helping you up the stairs. My stepmother is European and raised my brothers and me to open doors for women, walk on the street side of the sidewalk, offer a steadying arm on stairs and across streets."

She smiled pensively, probably thinking that he was odd. But he got that a lot, so he was used to it.

"And that's charming," she said. "But I'm quite agile."

"I'll remember that." He walked up the stairs beside her.

"I'm sorry this is wasting time you should be spending with your family," she said.

He shook his head. "I called and explained. We'll connect later. I'm surprised our paths have never crossed before. I'm at the hospital all the time. Are you new to Losthampton?"

"Ah...a couple of months." She gave him that look again. "I've been filling in on odd shifts. Fortunately, my neighbor will baby-sit any time I need her. You're there all the time as a patient, or for some other reason?"

"Sometimes as a patient," he admitted with a little laugh. "I'm sort of the Evel Knievel of Long Island. Or Abominable Abbott, as my brothers like to say."

She smiled. Her teeth were square and very white, the left front one overlapping the right just a little at the bottom. She seemed warm and kind, but he had the feeling she probably didn't smile very much.

"Abominable Abbott," she repeated. "That's a terrible way to go down in history."

"I don't think I'll make the history books."

Draper held the door open for her and ushered her through a small, crowded office to an even smaller office on the other side. The walls were green and all the furnishings gray. He frowned at Sawyer. "Apologize for holding you up," he said under his breath. "But we need to make a point here."

Sawyer nodded. "I agree."

"You making time with my little perps' mother?" Draper asked with a grin.

"Why?" Sawyer returned the grin. "Is it against the law?"

"The way you risk your life, it is. This pretty lady's got enough troubles with her imaginative children."

Draper moved ahead to take Sophie and the children to a waiting area with wooden chairs. As they sat down, Sophie in the middle and the children crowding close to her, Sawyer saw them in a new light.

Up until now, they'd been a surprising, somewhat fun diversion on an ordinary afternoon—if you didn't consider how Sophie had been frightened and how he'd been made to look like a completely gullible idiot. He loved children, and he liked women in his life—at least, on a temporary basis. Commitment to one would require a basic change in his life he wasn't ready to make.

Right now, his time and energy were focused on the Abbott Mills Foundation and the best dispersal of its funds. It was a heavy responsibility, and he took it to heart.

Added to that, life at Shepherd's Knoll had been very distracting lately. In the past month alone Killian had brought his bride back to Shepherd's Knoll after a three-month separation, Sawyer had been practicing a ski jump for the Children with Cancer fund-raiser and broken several ribs, Brian had saved his life and taken his place in the family as their half brother and China Grant had appeared on their doorstep the very day of Sawyer's accident and said she thought she was their sister, Abigail.

Suddenly the Abbott family's life had superseded

his personal life. He'd done his best to support Killian and Cordie's renewal of their marriage, to spend time with Brian and get acquainted with China. After all, he'd always felt responsible for her disappearance in the first place. That is, if she *was* Abby.

He pushed that thought away, trying to refocus on Sophie and her children. Understanding what was going on here was important to him. Helping anyone in trouble was a family commitment.

There was something particularly appealing about Sophie, Eddie and Emma. And he felt a curious compulsion to know more. While the children had done an inadvertently cruel thing, he had to admire the cleverness of their scheme.

And what had it been about marriage that had made Sophie Foster not want another husband? Maybe the guy had been a rat.

Sawyer had gotten the impression, when she'd told him her husband was gone, that she'd wanted to let the matter go at that—as though he'd simply walked away. Then Emma had added that he'd gone to heaven. The expression in Sophie's eyes had said she didn't think so.

Sawyer followed them to the row of chairs, determined to know more about Sophie. She was very pretty in a delicate way, yet she looked as if she'd struggled through or endured something difficult. He knew that being a mother required toughness. Chloe, his stepmother, was a beautiful, genteel woman who could be as hard as necessary when the situation warranted it. But she'd had his father to help until he'd died, then she'd had the support of her son and her stepsons.

Sophie had the love of her children, but he'd gathered from this afternoon's antics that she had her hands full keeping them from harm—or at least, incarceration.

She looked lonely.

He sat on the other side of Eddie just as a nearby office door opened. The police chief stood in the doorway, his expression severe. Until he saw the children. Then his posture relaxed and he said in a firm but quiet voice, "Edward and Emmaline Foster?"

Eddie raised his hand.

"Come in, please," he said. "And bring your mother and Mr. Abbott."

Sawyer knew Chief Albert Weston from the hospital board. He was average in height, but wide and balding, and he'd honed his police presence to a fine art. Sawyer had seen him talk to a knife-wielding man whacked out on drugs and alcohol for three hours. By the time the city had sent a hostage negotiator, Weston had the man in the back of a police car, sobbing out his rage over a lost girlfriend, a lost job, a lost life.

Weston's office was like a room in a law enforcement museum. He had photos and citations on the wall from his years as a police officer in the city. He'd come to Losthampton ten years ago.

On a shelf behind his desk were trophies from the Long Island Officers Bowling League, and taped to the wall was artwork his grandchildren had created. Sawyer knew he and his wife were raising a nine-year-old abandoned by their daughter, who was living with a musician somewhere in L.A.

Weston arranged four chairs in front of his desk

and put the children in the middle two. Eddie, who'd been smiling and generally unconcerned to this point, now looked big-eyed and worried. Emma climbed into Sophie's lap.

"My officers are very busy," Weston said, shuffling through the paperwork on his desk. "Just today, six officers have answered sixty-three calls. How many is that apiece, Edward?"

Eddie sat forward. "Um…ten," he replied, "and three left over."

The chief suppressed a smile. "That's right. One was a robbery of a couple of cars at the beach, one was a tourist stranded on the rocks, two were traffic accidents, one was a man having a heart attack, one was a domestic…" The chief stopped, realizing the boy wouldn't know what that meant. "I realize you don't understand that, but they all take a lot of—"

"I know what a domestic is," Eddie interrupted. His worried expression deepened. "It's when a dad beats up a mom. It happened to us a couple of times." Then he turned to Sophie with sudden concern, as though afraid he'd said the wrong thing.

The pink in her cheeks vanished, but she drew a breath and put a hand on Eddie's shoulder. "That's all right. I'm sure Chief Weston wants you to tell him the truth. And he wants you to understand that it's bad to waste the time of his police officers, because they have important things to do."

As Sawyer dealt with equal parts of rage and sadness, he saw the chief's jaw drop for an instant.

Eddie nodded. "I didn't think about that when I saw Sawyer in the market. I just thought about how you need to have a husband that's nice to you instead of mean, and how cool it'd be to have a dad who likes us. So me and Emma gave him the test.''

Sophie's eyes brimmed with tears, and Sawyer was very grateful that Chloe had drummed into all her sons the old-fashioned notion that gentlemen carried handkerchiefs, if not for themselves, for the ladies they took to sad movies or sandy benches at the beach.

He handed her a white square of linen with a gray monogram. As she turned to accept it, a tear spilled over.

''The test?'' the chief asked Eddie.

''Yeah. Our dad yelled a lot. And when my bike broke, Mom fixed it. When Emma got lost, Mom went to find her. When Gracie got in trouble at school—''

Sophie put a hand on his knee. ''He understands, Eddie.''

''Who's Gracie?'' the chief enquired.

''She's our big sister,'' Eddie said. ''She's ten. She's grumpy 'cause she doesn't have any boobs yet. She stayed to watch a Jennifer Lopez special with Kayla Spoonby across the road.'' Apparently thinking her whereabouts required explanation, he added, ''We don't have cable.''

The chief nodded gravely. ''I see. So, telling Sawyer…Mr. Abbott…that you were kidnapped was part of the test?''

''Yeah. 'Cause one time I heard Mom talking to Grandma Berry and she said she never wanted to get married again unless she could find someone who'd rescue the children. That's me and Emma and Gracie.

And *rescue* means save, right? So we had to see if he thought we were in trouble he'd save us."

The chief opened his mouth to respond, and obviously had no idea what to say. The boy had clearly misinterpreted what he'd heard, but cleverly created his own solution to what he perceived to be the problem.

Sophie groaned and put Sawyer's handkerchief to her eyes for a moment. Then she lowered it and took Eddie's hand.

"I meant…rescue you from not having a dad. From having to go to ball games with me instead of a dad. From Emma having no one to carry her on his shoulders, and from Gracie having no one to tell her she's pretty."

Eddie obviously didn't get that, either. "But, she's ugly," he said seriously.

Sophie laughed, which was a good thing. Even the chief seemed relieved. Sawyer wanted to take Sophie and her children away to Shepherd's Knoll, wrap them in fleece and shut out the world.

Of course, he knew that wasn't healthy. But he had to do *something*.

"Okay." The chief cleared his throat, then did it again. "Well. Now I understand what you were thinking when you scared your mother that way, but the next time you get an idea like that, I want you to promise me you'll think twice. You know what that means?"

"Think twice," Eddie repeated, considering. "Think about it two times so…so if there're bad parts in the idea, you'll see them."

"Exactly," the chief praised. "'Cause I'm sure

your mom worries about you all the time. Moms usually do. And there's enough real stuff to worry about without making things up that just scare people. Understand?''

"Yeah," Eddie said.

Weston focused on Emma. "Do you understand, Emmaline?"

She nodded. "We don't want to scare Mommy."

"That's right. Okay." The chief stood and shook hands all around. "I'll get an officer to take you back to your car."

"We had walked to the market," she said. "But if someone could take us home…"

"I'll do that." Sawyer shook the chief's hand.

"Mr. Abbott, maybe it'd be better…" She began to object to his plan, but the children skipped after him as he'd thought they might as he walked out of the chief's office, through the police station and down the steps to the parking lot. Sophie had little choice but to follow them.

He opened the back door of his deep-plum-colored PT Cruiser for Eddie and Emma and then scrambled in. They pulled on seat belts as he held the passenger door for Sophie.

"What if we all go out for pizza or burgers?" Sawyer suggested as he pulled out of the lot. "It's after seven. Kind of late for you to start cooking."

The children began a chorus of, "Please, Mommy! Can we? Please?" which he'd have caved to had he been in charge. But she was obviously made of stronger stuff.

"Thank you, but we have to go home," she said firmly. "Gracie's at the neighbor's, and—"

"Can't we just pick her up and take her along?"

Sophie shook her head. "No, but thank you."

Eddie and Emma whined a little louder. "We *never* get to do anything fun! We *never* get to go out to eat! We *never*—"

"You know the rule about whining," she interrupted.

Sophie was determined to get out of this without a further commitment or connection of any kind to Sawyer Abbott. As sweet and charming as he was, she wanted never to see him again. Ever.

"Which way home?" he asked as they reached the road that ran through Losthampton.

Funny, she thought. She'd been asking herself that question for years. When everything had gone bad with Bill, she'd sort of run in place for a long time, trying to find the road back to the way things had been before he'd fallen in with bad cops and become someone different from the man she'd married. She'd been lost in a nightmare for so long that when she finally escaped, she still felt as though she was getting nowhere.

The move from Boston to Losthampton had been intended to help her break free, to put Gracie in a new place, where the old memories would fade in the light of new experiences.

But Gracie was having as much trouble forgetting as Sophie was, so it felt as though they were still stuck in place.

Only Eddie and Emma provided the occasional breath of fresh air with their irrepressible good humor and direct approach to life. If she could just get through to them that their daddy search was hopeless.

She wondered idly if an uncle would appease them.

"Sophie," Sawyer prompted. "Which way?"

She was a little surprised to hear her name on his lips. There was something nice about hearing it quietly spoken rather than shouted at full volume with a threat in it.

Something inside her made her want to lean toward him, tell him how nice it would be to have pizza or burgers and feel certain that the need wouldn't erupt into an ugly event with the children crying and her wondering what on earth had happened to her life.

But life with Bill had changed her, and she had nothing left to give a man—even over pizza. So she just had to live with that, focus on her children and not mess up anyone else's life.

"We live on Blueberry Road," she said finally. "That old cottage right at the end."

"Oh, yeah." He turned in that direction. "I heard somebody'd moved into that place." He smiled apologetically. "Small-town rumor mill, you know. It's been vacant a long time."

"Yes. I cleaned up the living room and the kids slept there for two months until I could make their bedrooms livable. Now I'm slowly working on the rest of it."

"Nothing like an old house," he said. "Ours has been around since the mid-1800s. Belonged to my mother's family."

"Was your mother a native New Yorker?"

"She was from an old Texas family, actually. They used to summer here. Her great-grandfather built the place and called it Bluebonnet Knoll after the flowers from home. When she left with the chauffeur, she signed the place over to my father—to assuage her guilt, I suppose.''

Sophie *could* imagine running away, but from circumstances, not from the kids.

"How old were you?"

"Ah…three. Killian was five. Then my father married a designer who worked for one of his clothing companies, and they had two children together."

"Is Killian the brother you're meeting after you drop us off?"

"No, he and his wife are in Europe on a second honeymoon. I'm meeting Brian Girard. My mother was pregnant with him when she left."

"So he was the chauffeur's…?"

"No. His father is the owner of the neighboring estate."

"Good heavens!" She put a hand over her mouth to stop a smile. "I'm sorry. I know it isn't funny. It is your life, after all. But it sounds like a soap opera during Sweeps Week when they pull out all the stops to get the biggest audience share."

He didn't bother to hold back his smile. "There's more," he said. "Our little sister was kidnapped at fourteen months and we never saw her again. But about two weeks ago, a young woman appeared on our doorstep, who thinks she might be her."

"You're kidding!"

"I'm not. She's dark-haired like Campbell—that's my younger brother—and she and he squabble like real siblings, so I wouldn't be at all surprised if she is."

"Well…aren't you going to find out for sure?" she asked. "A DNA test would do it, wouldn't it?"

He nodded. "I think it will. But my stepmother's in France, looking after her dying aunt right now, and we don't want to do anything to upset her. So we haven't told her China is here, and we haven't gone for testing. China's in agreement. She's living at Shepherd's Knoll with us and helping Campbell run the estate."

"I thought it was Bluebonnet Knoll."

"My father changed the name when my mother left. Our ancestors raised sheep in Massachusetts before starting a mill, so Dad wanted the place to reflect his heritage rather than hers."

"How interesting," she said, "to be able to follow your ancestry so far back. All I know is that my grandparents farmed in Nebraska, lost everything in a drought and moved back to Vermont, where my great-grandfather was and the family's been there ever since."

He smiled. "What brought you here?"

"I spent ten years in Boston after I got married. We vacationed here one summer and I loved it."

She'd been telling everyone simply that she was a widow starting over. But he knew it wasn't that simple. Still—she didn't want him to know much more.

"Fresh start," she said, relieved as he turned onto Blueberry Road.

"Is there anything I can do?" he asked, glancing at her as he led the car down the long, straight road. "I mean…if you need anything for you or the children, I have connections everywhere."

He didn't appear to be boasting. "It's kind of you to offer," she replied, "but we're doing fine."

"I'm not doing fine," Emma said petulantly. "My cookies are still at the market."

Sophie groaned. "The groceries." She wondered if her cart had been set aside for her, or if everything had been put back. She hadn't had time to pay before the police had taken her and her children away.

"Well, you'll have to be happy with fruit for a snack tonight," she said. "We'll go back to the store tomorrow. And if you don't tell some stranger a made-up story about being kidnapped, maybe we won't have to go to jail and can actually take our groceries home."

"He's not a stranger," Eddie corrected. "He's The One."

Embarrassed by her children's insistence that they'd chosen the second son of the prominent and wealthy Abbotts to be their father, Sophie closed her eyes, completely out of excuses for their behavior.

"I could use that as billing for my next stunt," Sawyer laughed. "Sawyer Abbott—The One!" He gave the line dramatic flair as he turned into the driveway of her ramshackle but charming old house. The white paint was peeling and one gray shutter hung, but she was in love with the wide front porch and the window boxes, in which she'd planted yellow and purple pansies. The sight of them always cheered her.

She took a deep breath and faced Sawyer, prepared to thank him, then dismiss him.

But he was already out of the car, helping the children out of the back, looking over the house and the overgrown lawn. Eddie and Emma pranced along on either side of him, talking nonstop.

"Who's that?"

Gracie stood near the car door as Sophie let herself out. Beside her was Kayla Spoonby, her best friend. Kayla's father was the hospital administrator, and her mother, a schoolteacher.

Sophie recounted the story of the afternoon's adventures for Gracie and Kayla.

Gracie watched Sawyer Abbott with suspicion and hostility. "They're such dweebs. We don't need a dad."

"It's nice to have a dad," Kayla disputed. She was a short, plump redhead with a sparkling personality. Gracie was tall and slender, with her father's blond good looks but Sophie's shyness. "And Sawyer's really cool. He's a friend of my dad's. Hi, Sawyer!" she called, running around the car to greet him.

He opened his right arm for her, Eddie permanently attached to his left. Emma, obviously feeling left out, began to do cartwheels for attention.

Gracie stayed well out of the way, though Kayla called her over to introduce her. She gave Sawyer a half wave but took a step back when he started toward her.

He stopped, returned the wave, then braced himself as Emma cartwheeled right into him. She and Eddie tried to pull him toward the house. He resisted.

"Thank you so much," Sophie said hurriedly, peeling her children off him. "It was very kind of you not to be angry at them for ruining your evening. What do you say, Eddie?"

"That he's *The One!*" Eddie replied.

She should have known better than to be nonspecific. "What do you say to Mr. Abbott?"

"You're the—" he began.

"Eddie!"

Eddie held out his narrow hand. "Thank you," he said dutifully.

"And..." she prompted.

"And...I'm sorry?" He turned to her questioningly.

She nodded approval.

"I think," Eddie went on, "that it'd be really nice if we asked him to stay for dinner."

"Well, if we had something nice to feed him," she replied, relieved to have an excuse not to, "we'd do that, but our groceries are still at the store."

"Maybe he isn't fussy," Emma said, still holding his hand. She squinted up at him. "We have egg sandwiches when we don't have other stuff. Do you like that?"

Sophie would have countered with another excuse for why he couldn't stay, but Sawyer mercifully handled that for her. He got down on one knee, still holding each child's hand. "I really appreciate the invitation," he said with apparent sincerity, "but I promised to meet my brother for dinner and I'm already a little late. I'd really like it, though, if you invited me again sometime."

"How 'bout tomorrow?" Eddie offered quickly.

Sawyer smiled up at Sophie. "Maybe we should let your mom pick the time. She can call me when it would be convenient. Okay?"

"She won't do it," Emma said with a condemning glance at Sophie. "She'll say 'someday,' but she'll forget."

Sawyer grinned at that stain on her character, then

said, "Well, I'll just count on you two to remind her, okay?"

"Okay." Eddie shook his hand and Emma strangled him with a hug.

"Now, make sure you don't scare your mom anymore by disappearing on her," he said, looking at each of them solemnly. "And don't fib about her kidnapping you, even if you think you have a good reason. Lies are never good, okay?"

They nodded in unison.

Sawyer straightened, waved at Gracie again, wished Sophie good luck and went to his car.

Sophie felt a surge of relief as he drove away, then, when he was out of sight, a strange disappointment. He was the kind of man who could make her long for one in her life again. But she had too much against her now to know how to be happy with one. Bill had finally managed to convince her that it couldn't be done.

Gracie came to stand beside her as she stared at the empty road. It, too, could be a metaphor for her life.

"You don't *like* him, do you?" Gracie asked.

Sophie didn't even want to focus on that question sufficiently to answer it.

"He was very kind to us," she replied. "Most people would have been angry, but he brought us home, instead."

"He runs his family's foundation," Kayla said knowledgeably. "So, he kinda works for charities. He's nice all the time."

"Nobody's nice all the time," Gracie argued, turning toward the house.

Kayla patted Sophie's arm in a very sisterly way. Sophie often wondered how much of their personal history Gracie had shared with her best friend. "Once she knows how nice he really is," she said authoritatively, "she'll see that even though he's a man, he's not the way her dad was, and she'll get to like him, also." Then she grinned winningly at Sophie. "So you can fall in love if you want to. It's going to be okay."

Chapter Three

Brian's General Store and Boat Rental was a six-hundred-square-foot building typical of East Coast waterfront construction circa 1880. Its bright green board-and-batten front had faded to a comfortable mossy color. The natural-wood window boxes that graced the four-over-four windows were devoid of flowers at the moment. When Brian had bought the building, he'd removed the dead stalks that had been all that was left of the previous flowers, and hadn't found time yet to replace them.

Two benches, flanked by pots of flowers, stood on the porch on either side of an old carved front door. Sawyer remembered the cigar-store Indian that had stood there, a beautiful wooden carving that had fascinated the local children and tourists. But in the interest of political correctness, he'd been donated to the museum and replaced by a wooden fisherman in full Gloucester gear.

Sawyer climbed the wide steps and let himself into the store, ignoring the Closed sign. He knew Brian had left the door open for him.

Inside, the goods were arranged on shelves as old

as the building. In the middle of the floor was a pot-bellied stove with chairs pulled up to it. The former owner had used it to display sale merchandise, but Brian planned to use it for its intended purpose come winter.

Blue-and-white café curtains graced the windows and provided privacy for the small cubicle that served as a fitting room at the back. Near it in two old wooden wardrobes were a few items of clothing—Losthampton T-shirts and sweatshirts, a few light jackets for those who visited unprepared for the some-times cool nights. In the open drawers at the bottom was an assortment of the usual souvenirs—spoons, mugs, pencil cases. The same blue-and-white fabric also concealed a small office-cum-stockroom at the back.

Brian walked out from behind it as Sawyer rapped on the old wooden counter, also original to the store. A yardstick was nailed against the edge on the clerk's side from the days when yard goods were sold.

Sawyer had loved this store as a child, and couldn't quite believe that the brother he hadn't even known about in those days now owned it.

"Hey!" Brian greeted him, holding the curtain aside for him to join him in the back. "You get pa-roled?"

Brian was lean and long-legged, with the same dark blond hair and blue eyes Sawyer had, but with an angular line to chin and cheekbone that reminded Sawyer of Killian.

Sawyer knew there'd be jokes on the subject of his "scrape" with the law for some time to come. "They decided I was innocent after all. You ready?"

"Yeah. But are you sure you still feel like doing this?"

"Yes. But if you have other things to do, say so."

Because of an ongoing feud between their families over the years, Sawyer had been conditioned to think of Brian as an enemy. His new status as brother and friend was welcome but disorienting. Brian, too, seemed wary of it sometimes.

"I don't have anything else to do," Brian insisted. "It's just that it sounds like you've had a rough couple of hours and I don't want you to feel obligated...."

Sawyer drew an exasperated breath. Brian was beginning to remind him of Campbell and his conviction that he didn't *belong* in the Abbott family because he was from their father's second marriage. Considering that Sawyer and Killian both loved Chloe, Campbell's mother, and she was still very much the matriarch of their household, he had trouble figuring out where Cam's lack of confidence in his position came from.

"I don't feel obligated because you're my brother," Sawyer said with impatience, "but I do want to make up for lost time. We spent most of our lives fighting with each other, and that seems like a terrible injustice to me."

Brian looked momentarily startled, then said gravely, "I thought you'd feel obligated because I saved your life at great risk to my own, and I didn't want that. But if you want to feel obligated because you're my brother and you owe me a lifetime of doing things for me, taking the blame for me, helping me with difficult tasks, that's all right, too."

Sawyer stared at him, just beginning to understand

that Brian had what was proving to be a very Abbott sense of humor, even though their connection was on their mother's side of the family.

"You have me confused with Killian," Sawyer said finally. "I never did any of those things for Campbell, and I'm not doing them for you. But if you want help painting a few of the rental boats, I'm willing to do that in exchange for the fried clams you promised."

"You won't even help me with my rent now that my father's disowned me?"

"I happen to know you got this place for a song, and that you inherited your grandmother's house free and clear."

Brian blinked at Sawyer's bald refusal. "What about my wounded sense of self-worth?"

"We're all dealing with that one. You'll just have to keep up."

"You won't even help me find a woman now that Killian has the only one I ever cared about?"

Brian was acquainted with Cordelia, Killian's wife, since college, before she knew Killian. Because Brian's family had always been in competition, businesswise, with the Abbotts, the children had grown up enemies. Brian had enjoyed flirting with Cordie to hurt Killian and civilities had been strained—until they'd learned Brian and the Abbotts were related.

"Ah. I may be willing to help you there. I do seem to have something that makes them flock to me."

"It's money," Brian said, digging his keys out of his pocket.

"I thought it was charm and wit."

"I'm sorry. It's not. Come on, we'll take my car

to Yvonne's.'' Yvonne made the best fried clams in the Hamptons.

Sawyer climbed into Brian's new black pickup. He'd traded in his Porsche for it as a sign of dedication to his new life. "Younger brothers," he said, "are supposed to be respectful and blinded by hero worship."

Brian grinned at him as he slid in behind the wheel. "You should have explained that to me before I agreed to this whole brother thing." They roared away.

It was almost midnight by the time Sawyer got home. They'd put a coat of paint on three of the small boats Brian had acquired with the rental part of the business, then had a beer on the front porch before going their separate ways.

Sawyer had enjoyed Brian's company, and was surprised by how connected he felt to him despite the lifetime spent at odds. And though he made light of it, he knew Brian had come to his rescue without hesitation that day on the water when Sawyer's waterskiing stunt had gone wrong, and he would always feel indebted for that.

As Sawyer walked into the house, it was clear that someone was quarreling with someone else. One of the raised voices coming from the living room was male, the other female.

Winfield greeted Sawyer at the door. He was sort of a butler-bodyguard Campbell had hired last year, convinced their security was lax. Winfield was built like a tank, had a voice like a grinding motor and possessed a gentle nature completely at odds with his appearance.

"They're at it again," he said, closing the door.

"What are they fighting about?"

"Not sure. Anything and everything."

"I'll go see what I can do."

Sawyer would have just let them have at it as Killian had advised when it was obvious, the day of China's arrival at Shepherd's Knoll, that the two were not going to get along. But if she *was* Abigail, and they'd been without her all this time, it was criminal that warfare should ensue when she'd finally been restored to them.

And if she *wasn't* Abigail, then he was still in sympathy with her.

Campbell had voted against letting her stay until Chloe came home, convinced she was lying for purposes of her own, but Sawyer and Killian had outvoted him. That had happened a lot in his life because of their different personalities rather than their different mothers, but all Campbell knew was that he often lost to his elder brothers. This time, it seemed, he didn't mind taking his frustrations out on China.

Sawyer found them standing toe-to-toe in the large living room. Campbell, tall and dark-haired, with Chloe's milk-chocolate eyes and fine-boned face, had more of an air of aristocracy than did Killian and Sawyer combined. Add to that his sense of loss and his moody personality had all the stuff of a Gothic hero.

China, on the other hand, exuded cheerful practicality, and had little patience for the drama he brought to every moment. She was average in height, with a slender grace that reminded him of Chloe. Or it could be a simple femininity many women had in common.

Her long hair was caught at the back of her neck with a chased silver clip.

"I *didn't* forget to take a message," she was saying with hot annoyance as Sawyer approached them. "I told you! I put it with the stack of mail Kezia put aside for you on the hall table. If you lost it after that, it isn't my fault."

Campbell was pulled up to full-pride height, but maintained his cool flawlessly. Only Sawyer, who fought with him often, recognized the tight muscle in his jaw.

"Had you done that," he said, "it would have been there when I picked up my mail."

"Had you come home that night," she retorted, "instead of partying, it might still have been there, instead of possibly blowing off when someone walked by or opened the door."

"Maybe you should have put it in my hand, and not on top of my mail, so that it wouldn't have blown off!" he said darkly. "I alerted everyone that I was expecting a call back from the Barrow estate and that it was important."

"That would have required my being in your presence," she snapped back, "and that's usually a regrettable experience!"

"Whoa!" Sawyer caught her arm as she would have stormed off. "I happen to know that Kezia put that message on your computer keyboard," he said to Campbell, "because she knew how important it was to you. But you never close your door against Versace."

Versace was Cordie's cat, left in their care while she and Killian were second-honeymooning. He was fat and gray, his long coat making him look the size of a spaniel. He was also mean-tempered, and spent long hours on the porch swing since Cordie had been gone. "I've seen him sleeping on your desk more than once. He might have knocked it off. Check under and around the desk."

"Thank you," Campbell said grudgingly.

"Sure."

To China, Campbell said with what seemed to require superhuman effort, considering the way he squared his shoulders and drew a breath, "I'm sorry."

"Oh, you are not," she disputed. "I have tried to be polite, but you resent me, and now I'm not wild about the thought that we could be related, either. Let's just agree to dislike each other. I'm comfortable with that."

Campbell shook his head at Sawyer. "This can't be the little sister we've missed all these years."

Sawyer had to smile at that. "You don't really know what it's like to have a younger sibling because we didn't have her very long. But however you've idealized that relationship, what you two are experiencing now is much closer to reality. Younger siblings are always making your life difficult."

Campbell turned to China with an aggrieved expression. "Heaven help me."

She muttered a scornful sound. "I think you're looking for help in the wrong direction. Good night, Sawyer." She stalked off toward the stairs.

Campbell groaned as though he'd taken all he could take. "It would be so satisfying to hit her on the head with a Tonka truck."

Sawyer thought it interesting that he'd said that because he and baby Abigail had fought over just that the day she'd disappeared. He knew Campbell remembered because he'd mentioned it once or twice. Abby had crawled into his room, and while he was usually patient with her, he'd been in a mood that day and had yanked his truck away from her when she'd tried to play with it. Chloe had removed her, scolding Campbell for not being more understanding.

Abby had returned later that afternoon and he'd put her bodily in the hallway and closed the door in her face.

"While you could have gotten away with that at five and a half," Sawyer warned, "you'd be in a lot of trouble these days if you behaved that way. And I wouldn't want to make her really mad. Your mother's ancestors sailed with Lafitte, remember?"

"I have the same blood," Campbell reminded him. "I'm a match for her. God, she's all attitude."

"I suppose it's hard to be agreeable with someone when you know he hates you."

"I don't hate her," Campbell was quick to deny. "I just don't like her—a *lot*."

Sawyer couldn't help but ask. "Why is that, anyway?"

"I don't trust her," Campbell replied without even having to think about it. "She's not Abby."

"How do you know?"

Campbell looked upstairs and said in a pained and puzzled tone, "Because Abby wouldn't hate *me*."

Sawyer didn't know how to respond. That reply was indicative of the complex workings of Campbell's mind and the deep mysteries it held. Did he really expect the behavior of a twenty-six-year-old woman to reflect the affections of a child he hadn't seen in twenty-five years? Somehow, he did.

"I think I should take the DNA test," he said, "and be done with it."

They'd all agreed that wasn't wise when she'd first arrived. "Come on, Cam. We don't want to do that to Mom."

"If she isn't Abby," Campbell argued, "we get rid of her before Mom even has to know she was here."

"And if she is Abby," Sawyer countered, "Mom missed the discovery of her daughter's return. And would China stay if she *knew* the test would prove she wasn't our sister?"

"Why not? Everyone's been treating her like royalty. She'd want to keep it up as long as she could. Then, when the test proves she isn't Abby, she can just claim she didn't know."

"How do you explain all the Abbott Mills things she found in her box?"

Campbell sighed. "I don't. I try hard to remember the night she disappeared, but all that comes to me is the nanny screaming, Mom crying, Dad not talking to anybody for days. And I remember you and me climbing into Killian's bed and talking about running away to find her. But Killian said we shouldn't 'cause Mom and Dad were already too upset."

Campbell drew back from the memories suddenly and rubbed a hand over his eyes. "I'm going to see if I can find that message."

"Do you think you got the job?" Sawyer asked. Campbell was always applying for jobs on other estates, convinced he'd never truly discover himself until he was out from under the influence of Killian and Sawyer.

"No idea." Campbell stretched both arms and yawned. "At interviews, I think I make a good impression, but when the question comes down to why I'd want to leave Shepherd's Knoll for another position, it's a tough one to explain without getting into a lot of personal stuff, and I think they all begin to believe there has to be something wrong with me."

"There is," Sawyer confirmed. "You're nuts."

Campbell accepted that assessment with a. nod. "Thanks, bro. Just the vote of confidence I needed." He started to walk away, then turned back again as though he'd just remembered something. "How was your dinner with Brian?"

"Good," Sawyer said. "You should have come."

"I had to go over China's work on the house budget before I pay bills tomorrow."

"How'd she do?"

"Very well," Campbell admitted in mild surprise. "She seems to have a good grasp of what it takes to keep the place going, though I'll have to explain Mom to her."

When Killian suggested that China work with Campbell until Chloe came home, Campbell had given her the job he hated most—the household accounts. Chloe was a little bit of a spendthrift and cheerfully defied any and all efforts to make her account for her purchases, insisting that their father never had. It made organizing the books difficult.

For the representative of a charity to appear with a handwritten note from Chloe promising a sizable donation wasn't at all unusual. Sawyer had tried to remind her that that was what the foundation was for, and with better controls, but she would just dismiss his objections with a very Gallic wave of her hand and do it again the following week. With foundation funds committed to distribution in a very particular way, such donations were paid for out of the household money.

Then there was the time she replaced her bedroom furniture and wrote a check for it the same day Campbell had paid the staff, the car insurance, the utilities and the quarterly taxes.

Kezia's paycheck had bounced. Fortunately, she'd understood her employer's foibles and explained the problem to Campbell, who had promptly covered it for redeposit. Sawyer hated to think what could have happened. Facing down a bounced check at the IRS would have been bad enough, but having the car insurance expire the way Cordie drove might have been disastrous.

"It's weird to think Brian's related to us," Campbell said. "Well, to you."

Killian and Sawyer were always annoyed when Campbell made the distinction between the first half of the family and the second half, insisting they were all one whole. But Killian generally replied to that with reassurance if not always with patience, while Sawyer tended to accuse Campbell of trying to create differences where there weren't any. As stand-in eldest when Killian was gone, Sawyer tried to react as he would have.

"We're all connected, if not directly related," he said, thinking that sounded flimsy. However, the situation was odd. Brian shared Sawyer and Killian's mother, but not their father, and therefore had no genetic ties at all to Campbell. "He has to feel it, too. Once he knew, he protected us from making an investment that would have allowed his father to get a foothold in Abbott Mills—something he's been after for a long time, and would ultimately have hurt us significantly."

Campbell nodded. "I know. Maybe he'll take some of the heat off me with Killian. If he's wanting in while I'm moving out, I'll get less flack about needing to find my own space."

"Yeah, right. If you're thinking Brian will replace you in our minds, he won't. He's far less difficult to get along with than you are, and generally more laid-back. We'll notice the calm the moment you're out the door."

Campbell rolled his eyes at him. "If I don't get China attuned to the way Mom uses the checkbook, you'll all be out the door and looking for employment. And I understand you're in trouble with the law already. Kezia said you called her to tell her something about being arrested for kidnapping?"

"I wasn't arrested," Sawyer corrected, and recounted the story.

"And their mother wasn't angry at you?" Campbell asked in amazement.

He shook his head. "I couldn't quite believe it, either."

"Mmm. That old Sawyer charm struck again, I suppose."

"Actually, it went down in flames. She told me in no uncertain terms not to call."

"She's had it with men?" Campbell speculated.

"Did you explain that you never get serious about women? That you have a death-defying approach to life and don't want anything to distract you from it?"

Sawyer frowned at his brother's psychoanalysis of him. "She had an abusive husband, I think. And her ten-year-old daughter kept a clear distance from me. I suppose if you've experienced that kind of thing, every man is suspect."

"But you said the little kids liked you."

"Yeah."

Campbell studied Sawyer. "So…you liked her, or you sympathized with her plight?"

"Both, I guess. And she's very pretty."

"Do you need that kind of trouble?"

Sawyer grinned. "I thrive on trouble."

"You thrive on danger. Subtle difference. Good night."

"Good night," Sawyer replied, thinking his brother had a good point.

Campbell stopped halfway up the stairs. "Did anybody tell you your in-line skates arrived? What's the stunt this time?"

Sawyer grinned. All right! "Just in the planning stages. Where are they?"

"On the hall table with the mail. Unless Versace got to them, too."

Chapter Four

Sophie hammered a nail into a loose stair, second from the bottom, on the front porch.

"If we had a dad," Eddie said casually, eating an orange Popsicle that now coated all parts of his face, "you wouldn't have to do this kind of stuff."

"I'm good at this kind of stuff." That wasn't entirely true, but she *could* hammer in a nail. And she'd been fending off the children's examples of how their household would be better served with a man in it since the incident two days ago. To make matters worse, Sawyer Abbott had returned to the market after he'd left them, retrieved their groceries and deposited them on the front porch. Gracie had responded to a knock on the door and seen him driving away.

"Mommy, you nailed Hermione to the step!" Emma complained as she tried to pick up her redheaded rag doll, named after Harry Potter's friend.

It was true. Several loops of her hair had been caught by the nail. Now Sophie was faced with having to undo her work or bargain with her daughter for a radical step in Hermione's hair care. And Emma was a tough negotiator.

"What if we snip the loops that are caught," she suggested, "and tie them back with one of your barrettes?"

Emma considered that a moment, then looked up with a gleam in her eye. "Then I'll need a new barrette." Emma was always angling for something for her hair—a passion she'd caught from her elder sister.

The maneuver was manipulative, but it made this moment easier and Sophie was happy to concede. "I guess you do."

"Okay."

"Sawyer has cool hair," Eddie said as they all stood at the kitchen counter while Sophie fastened a barrette in Hermione's red wool bob.

Sophie preferred traditional good grooming, but she had to admit that Sawyer Abbott's dark blond spiked style had been somehow…cute. Truth be told, she'd thought about him a lot in the past two days, but she'd spent at least as much time reminding herself that she and her children were fine as they were. She had to raise them safely to adulthood before she could think about herself. They'd been through enough already.

Still, she felt herself drift away in her mind from the confining borders of her little life. She imagined what it would be like to date a man whose purpose was learning about a woman rather than controling her.

She imagined what it would be like to enjoy a picnic, a dinner out or even a quiet dinner at home without being on the very edge of her nerves, wondering when the smiling charm and consideration would turn into unreasonable anger over the smallest, sometimes fabricated provocation.

She was just beginning to unwind from the last few nightmare years of her marriage, just beginning to feel safe from imminent danger. But a part of her had been closed away by those years, and in self-protection, she'd thrown away the key.

The only way to feel completely secure was to accept her sexual solitude and live for the children. She understood that.

She was just surprised to find herself longing for things she was so sure she'd never want again.

"We could ask Sawyer to come to dinner tomorrow night," Eddie suggested, a little drama in his voice intended to convince her the thought had just occurred to him. Of course he'd proposed that several times yesterday, and before she'd left for work this morning.

"Mom has to work tomorrow night." Gracie walked into the kitchen with Kayla, who was staying with them tonight while her parents went to the theater in New York City. "And we don't want a father, so stop trying to force one on us."

"He doesn't *have* to be a dad," Eddie argued. "He could just be a boyfriend. Rusty Martin's mom has lots of them."

"Rusty Martin's mom is a—" Kayla began.

"A very nice lady," Sophie interrupted quickly, handing Emma back the doll, "who lost her husband and Rusty's little sister in a car accident, so I think we can be kind and not pass judgment on her."

"What's 'pass judgment'?" Eddie asked.

"Decide who's good and who's bad," Sophie replied. "Sometimes people do things that look bad just because they're confused...or lonely."

Gracie and Kayla studied her doubtfully. Sherri Martin did have a well-deserved reputation as a woman who slept around, but Sophie knew from first-hand experience that the judgments people made could be completely wrong. Several of her friends had stopped offering help when it became clear Bill was abusive and she was remaining in the marriage.

They didn't know how hard it was for her to give up on the man Bill had once been, and the love they'd once shared so openheartedly before power and the underside of crime in Boston had changed him. When it became clear to her that that was gone forever and she'd tried to leave, his protective connections at the police department had "misdirected" her 911 calls, tracked her when she ran, helped him thwart her at every turn.

"The way she appears to live isn't right at all," she told the girls firmly, afraid they'd misunderstand her message here, "but it isn't up to us to call her names. You just never know why people do what they do."

Emma mercifully brought the conversation to a safer place. "How come you have to work tomorrow night, Mommy?"

At last. Something she could explain directly. "Because one of the swing-shift nurses broke her leg and they're getting somebody to replace her, but I have to cover for her tomorrow night."

"Could we get back to the boyfriend thing?" Eddie asked.

"Mom doesn't want a boyfriend, either," Gracie

said, glancing at Sophie for corroboration. For the first time since Sophie and her daughter had become allies in that belief, Sophie's conviction wavered just a little. Gracie must have seen that in her eyes and widened hers. "Mom, you promised," she reminded quietly.

"Promised what?" Eddie asked.

"That she'd never get married again," Gracie put in quickly, anxiously. "That there'd never be anybody else around to be mean to us. Like a dad or a boyfriend."

The warring camps stared at each other from opposite sides of the table—Eddie and Emma on one side, Gracie on the other. Kayla remained neutral, though she stood beside her friend.

"Well, it's two to one!" Eddie said with playground justice in his corner. "And we want a dad."

"Dads can be good," Kayla said as she had the night Sawyer had brought them home.

"And they can be mean," Gracie insisted. "They can yell and make you scared and slam doors and throw things!"

Kayla, who'd obviously never experienced such things, folded her arms, remaining firm. "Yeah. But most of them aren't like that. Some of them don't pay much attention to you, but they never hurt you. Some of them work all the time, but are really nice to you when they're around, and some of them, like my dad, love you a whole bunch. They yell sometimes, and they get mad when you mess up, but they're not mean. They even like having you around."

"I bet Sawyer would be like that," Eddie said.

Gracie's defensive anger changed to a more complex sadness. "Yeah," she agreed grimly. "Our dad was like that. Then he changed. How can you be sure someone won't change?"

Kayla opened her mouth to reply, then seemed to realize she didn't have an answer.

Gracie turned to Sophie. "How would you know someone won't change?"

Sophie had to admit, "You don't." But knowing she had to put her wounded daughter on the right road as she approached adolescence, she said with conviction, "I think you have to trust people, until you have reason not to. And that means you have to be the smartest person you can be. How you see boys and men treat the other people in their lives is a good indicator of how they'll treat you."

Gracie nodded, her eyes welling with tears. "Daddy used to be nice to us when I was little."

Sophie went around the table toward her, needing to touch her, to feel closer. "He always loved all of you."

"He pushed me down when I tried to help you." Tears rolled down Gracie's cheek.

Sophie put an arm around her shoulder. "He didn't mean to do that. He was mad at me, and he didn't want you to be close enough to get hurt, so he pushed you away."

Gracie shook her head, memories of that night clearly torturing her. Bill had been shouting at Sophie about an expenditure for school clothes. He'd been involved for about a year by then with several other cops who were skimming the money taken from drug busts, and shaking down pimps and runners for protection. She'd been ignorant of those things at the time, but suspected he was into something. The transformation from good man and good cop to bad cop and dangerous man had been under way for a while.

Curiously, his own dissolution seemed to require blaming her, cutting her off from friends, narrowing her spending power. He'd closed their credit accounts, insisted she direct-deposit her check from the hospital where she worked, and kept a close eye on all purchases made with their debit card.

She'd been in touch with a rape-and-abuse counselor she'd seen advising victims at the hospital. The counselor had told her to prepare to leave and she'd find shelter for her and the children.

That particular day, Sophie had gotten an extra hundred dollars in cash from a debit-card purchase and stashed it as she planned her escape. He'd taken issue with the amount she'd spent; she'd argued; he'd slapped her; and when Gracie had come to her defense, he'd pushed his daughter away.

She'd fallen into the sharp corner of the coffee table and scraped her upper arm. He'd been horrified. Despite the monster he'd become, he'd never turned on the children except to shout, happy instead to take his aggressions out on Sophie.

Seeing Gracie's stunned and hurt expression, he'd left the house. Sophie patched Gracie up, called the counselor, and was gone with the children within an hour.

Sophie hid out for a year, evading all the means Bill had at his disposal to track her down. They'd settled happily into a crisis shelter, where someone was brought in to home-school the children.

Then one rainy April night when Bill and his partner were in pursuit of a couple of kids who'd robbed a woman at an ATM, their unit was struck by a freight truck at an intersection, and Bill and his partner were killed.

She'd felt terrible grief for the love she and Bill had once shared, then for the marriage that could now never be repaired. Not that she'd realistically held out any hope for that, but in her pain she recognized it as a need she'd suppressed, and she mourned for it, too.

She'd comforted her children while they'd wept, then realized that she was suddenly free of the shackles of fear and dread. The nightmare of her marriage was over.

"I think it'd be better," Gracie said, "if we just didn't have to worry about having a dad around. Then we know we'll be okay."

Sophie thought it hard to fault that reasoning. It was cowardly, but it made perfect sense.

"I may never see Sawyer Abbott again," Sophie said as she kissed Gracie's forehead, then reached into a drawer and retrieved a handful of place mats. "So, I don't think adding a man to the family is anything we need to worry about right now. Let's think about dinner, instead." She handed the place mats to Gracie, then retrieved the jug of milk from the refrigerator.

Familiar with their routines after eating dinner with them several times a week, Kayla got glasses out of an overhead cupboard. Emma took napkins from the middle of the table and began folding them into neat triangles. Eddie, in charge of condiments, waited for instructions.

"Butter and ketchup," Sophie directed as she removed a meat loaf from the oven and prepared to mash potatoes.

"What's the vegetable?" Eddie asked with a wince while he carried the butter tub and bottle of ketchup to the lazy Susan in the middle of the table.

"Broccoli," Sophie replied, and knew without turning that all four children stuck out their tongues. When she served corn, instead, a cheer rose around the table.

"It's starchy and not as good for you as broccoli," she preached, then smiled, "but it is great with meat loaf."

And making her children happy—except for finding Eddie and Emma a father—was what her life was all about.

SHE REMEMBERED HER REMARK about probably never seeing Sawyer Abbott again the following night when three teenage boys in T-shirts and shorts, bike helmets and knee pads brought him into the ER. It was shortly after 9:00 p.m., and she was charting notes to pass on to the next shift.

She recognized his voice immediately. "I'm okay," he was saying to the two anxious boys lending support on either side of him. "I was only out for a second."

"My dad's a doctor." The third boy, carrying what must have been Sawyer's helmet, advised, "Any head trauma should be looked at. That's what he says."

"Ha!" Sawyer teased. "You just like saying *head trauma* 'cause you think it makes you look smart."

"I *am* smart," the boy countered. "I didn't fall."

Sophie went to meet them as the admittance clerk led the group into the ER, grumbling to Sawyer that he should be in a wheelchair.

The boy carrying the helmet came forward. "His Glasgow Coma Score is 15," he said gravely. "I don't think he's in trouble, but we thought we should check." At her look of surprise that he knew the criteria for checking cognitive responses in someone with a head injury, he added, "I'm Henry Brown. Dr. Brown is my father."

"Ah," she said. Dr. Brown was an ER doctor. "Well, let's see how right you are. Let's get Mr. Abbott to this bed." She indicated the nearby gurney and propped up the back so he could sit up.

He seemed pleased to see her, his eyes bright with recognition. Or shock. She had to make sure before allowing herself this little feeling of pleasure at the sight of him.

"Mrs. Foster," he replied, "you're an injured man's dream. Does this Glasgow thing determine my Scottishness? Because I think there was a grandmother on my father's side—"

She knew he was being silly. "What's your name?" she asked, putting her fingertips to his pulse.

"Alistair MacDougal." At her scolding glance, he grinned. "I wanted to get 100 on the Glasgow thing." When she didn't smile but continued to monitor his pulse, he sighed dispiritedly, "Sawyer Jacob Abbott. I'm at Losthampton Hospital. I'm thirty-five. My address is…"

She let him go on while she determined that his pulse was strong and steady and his pupils were equal and reactive. She was about to put her stethoscope to her ears, when he said, "And your phone number is…" He rattled it off perfectly. At her astonishment, he said with a smile intended to charm, "I was going to call you about going to a movie this weekend. And you really should go out with me, because I imagine I'm going to need observation," he said, his litany of facts finally completed. "How long's your shift?"

"I thought you said you were fine."

"That was before I knew you were on duty."

"I'm off in an hour," she said. "I guess someone else will have to observe you."

"Then I *am* fine. Want to have a cup of coffee?"

"Dude," one of the boys said, shaking his head, "you don't expect to score with that line?"

Sawyer glanced grimly at the boys, then back to Sophie. "Do you have a shot that would make them disappear? You let them teach you to in-line skate the gravity wall and they think they own you. 'Bend your knees,'" he mimicked in a young voice. "'Turn at the waist. Maybe you're just too *old!*' I tell you, they're like a trio of old maids."

The boys ignored his diatribe. "He *is* too old," one of them said to Sophie. She thought he looked familiar. "He can't bend deep enough to get the right aerodynamics to get into the somersault with enough momentum to do a 360." The boy suddenly studied her more closely, then his eyes went to the name on her badge. "S. Foster," he said. "Sophie! You helped my mom and my sister and me at the safe house." He put a bony hand to his chest. "Jeff Howard?"

"That's right!" She remembered him now. He'd been quiet and angry and she'd talked to his mother about getting him into the Boys Bunker, a social and athletic club manned by counselors and teachers. The boys met in an old gym, where they worked out and played basketball and volleyball. "You must have grown six inches since I saw you last."

He grinned, clearly proud of that accomplishment. "Maybe. Everyone around me is shrinking." He grinned again at Sawyer. "'Specially the old guy. We met at the Bunker. He helps out there and he paid me and Stretch and Henry to teach him to do a 360 in the air on Rollerblades." He shook his head pityingly. "We're going to have to ask for more money."

Sawyer made a sound of distress. "Can he talk to an invalid like that?"

Sophie shooed the boys toward the waiting area. "Cafeteria's closed, but there're pop and candy machines near the outside door. Give me a little while to make sure the old guy is okay. Tell the clerk who brought you in that I said to let you use the phone to call your parents and let them know where you are."

Stretch, tall and gangly, with bright red hair, held up a cell phone. "We're covered. Please tell us if he croaks or something. We're going to divvy up his gear."

Sawyer pretended to leap off the table. Sophie pushed against his chest as the boys left, laughing.

"Seems you've endeared yourself to them, too," she said, putting a blood-pressure cuff on him. "Did you send their parents to jail, also?"

"What does a man have to do to get sympathy around here?" he complained; then, as she pumped the cuff, he asked, "You're imagining that around my neck, aren't you?"

She held up a finger for silence.

He made a face but complied.

She logged his blood pressure, thinking he was in better shape than most athletes.

"Am I going to live to show these boys that you can do a 360 at thirty-five?"

"By all appearances," she replied. "But Dr. Brown should look at you." She pulled a light blanket over him, careful not to touch him, and wandered away.

SHE WAS A CHARMING SIGHT in blue scrubs, the top sprigged with violets. She seemed about nineteen from the back, her saucy ponytail swinging as she walked. Sawyer found it hard to believe that she had three children and had endured a cruel husband. He couldn't imagine any man wanting to hurt a woman like that—or any woman.

He'd often wondered why women stayed in such circumstances, but even knowing her just a little, having witnessed her gentleness with her children, her consideration of him when he'd caused her a great deal of trouble, she had to have a reason that just wasn't apparent to him.

A doctor a little older than he was, but with a formidable paunch and bifocals, came to check him out.

After giving Sawyer several tests, then sending him off to Radiology for a CAT-scan, he amassed the results and grew chatty. "Looking good," he said. "Henry's my son, you know. He told me to do a good job with you."

"Nice kid." Sawyer sat quietly while the doctor made notes on his chart. "He's always quick to help put up or take down equipment, help another kid."

The doctor shook his head in mystification. "That's amazing, but I'm happy to hear it. At home he's a vegetable."

"I guess that's pretty typical."

"Mmm. I'm grateful for the Bunker. I work long hours and his mother's been gone two years. I'm glad he's hanging out somewhere safe."

"It's a great facility."

"Yes, it is. Now—how do we make sure *you* hang out someplace safe so you don't really hurt yourself next time? Foster showed me your chart, and I've read about you a couple of times in the paper. You're an accident that's *already* happened over and over. Why is that?"

Surprised by the doctor's apparent determination to talk about Sawyer's propensity for danger, he had to think a minute. "Well. I do it for charity. It raises—"

The doctor cut him off with a nod. "I know. People will flock to a spectacle. Even pay money to witness it, particularly when life and limb are at stake. But certainly there are other ways to raise money."

"Actually," Sawyer said, "this is quite effective."

The doctor ignored that. "It risks your life, Mr. Abbott," he said. "I doubt any of the charities you help with money would sacrifice you and all you do for them just to make a little more on your stunts. Particularly this hospital."

When Sawyer opened his mouth to argue further, the doctor silenced him with "Yes. It's none of my business, but you might want to talk it over with yourself sometime. Explore why you really do it." He stood and shook Sawyer's hand. "You're in good

health, Mr. Abbott, but if you develop a bad head-
ache, double vision, come right back.''

"Okay." Sawyer was relieved that conversation
was over.

"Foster volunteered to drive you home," the doctor added.

Sawyer sat up a little straighter. "Pardon me?"

"Foster," the doctor said again. "The nurse who
helped you when you arrived. She's off duty and volunteered to drive you home. I know Stretch drove you
over from the park, but his mother has to have the
car to go to work tonight, so he has to get home. He's
dropping off Henry and Jeff.''

Sawyer nodded, unable to believe tonight might
take a positive turn after all. "Okay. That's…great."

"She does know you, right?" The doctor teased
loudly enough for Sophie to hear as she approached
in street clothes, a big tan pouch purse slung over her
shoulder. "This isn't just a case of patient kidnap?"

Sophie pretended to think about that. "That didn't
occur to me. You're probably very ransomable, Mr.
Abbott.''

He shook his head as he slid off the bed and
reached to a nearby chair for his sweatshirt. "Not
when my mother's out of the country. My brothers
would let me go down without a second thought."

Sophie smiled at the doctor and said good-night.

Sawyer followed her through the double glass
doors out into the parking lot. The night was starlit
and smelled of flowers and saltwater, enough of a
breeze stirring that he pulled on his sweatshirt. He
didn't entirely understand this impulse to just sit with
her and talk, but it wouldn't be ignored. He just

wanted to help. That was what his life was all about—seeing that financial help got to the right places. Well, this wasn't a financial matter, but he was sure the same "help principle" applied. She needed a friend.

"You're sure you won't consider that cup of coffee?" Sawyer asked.

"You should get right home," Sophie said, marching along ahead of him toward a burgundy, American-made four-door sitting under a light, all alone on that side of the lot.

"The doctor said I'm fine."

"Head trauma often causes problems later."

"Everyone will be asleep at home," he argued practically. "When I'm with you, I'm in the company of a nurse."

She unlocked the car with the remote and smiled at him across the roof as he walked around to the passenger side. "I'm taking you home," she said firmly.

"Scared, huh?" he challenged. He was out of options.

Her frown told him that he couldn't trick her that way. "I used to be," she replied gravely. "All the time. But not anymore. Please get in the car."

Now he felt guilty for that careless remark. "I'm sorry," he said, slipping into the passenger seat. "That was thoughtless. I'd just like to get to know you better. You might even like getting to know me."

"Mr. Abbott." She inserted her key in the ignition, then gave him her full attention. She looked a little weary but very beautiful. "I appreciate your interest, and after three children, I'm even flattered by it. But I assure you I'm not relationship material. Please believe me when I say that." She buckled her belt and started the car.

"Everyone is relationship material," he argued as he snapped his seat belt into place. "Isn't there supposed to be someone for everyone?"

"Maybe. But I'm not the someone for you."

"You can't say that with any credibility without knowing me."

She drove slowly across the dark parking lot, then stopped before turning onto the road. She faced him again, clearly losing patience. "I don't *want* to know you better," she said firmly. "I'm sorry if that's harsh, but you don't seem to be able to take no for an answer."

"Well...a nurse is a sort of scientist, isn't she?" He was grasping at straws. "Conclusion without data is a very unscientific approach to anything."

"I know what I'm doing."

"How can you when you don't know *me?*"

"Because I know myself!" she shouted at him, then put a hand to her face and groaned. Then she slapped that hand to the steering wheel and frowned at him. "I apologize. I never yell. I hate that. Please," she pleaded. "Trust that I know what's best here."

She was going to hate this, so he said it carefully. "But if we're both involved, I should have some say in what's best for me, shouldn't I?"

"Okay, that's it!" She looked both ways, then burst out onto the street and sped to the next stop. Then, when he was sure he'd blown it and she was taking him back to the skating park at top speed, she made for the highway and the Night Owl Diner. It was open all night, as the name implied. "Sawyer, you leave me no choice. I'll explain to you why this will never work, then you'll wish you'd listened to me in the first place!''

''Fair enough,'' he said.

She dug blindly into her purse without taking her eyes away from the road and retrieved a cell phone. She hit two keys, then held the phone to her ear.

''Molly, hi, it's Sophie. Yeah. I'm going to be a little late. No, I'm fine, I'm just going to have a cup of coffee before I come home.''

Sawyer could hear a lively voice on the other end of the line.

''Molly...Molly, calm down,'' Sophie said. ''No, no. Just coffee. Are the kids okay?'' She listened a moment. ''Oh, good. They love the *Back to the Future* movies. Yeah, I'll be home in half an hour. Yes, it is. It's plenty long enough. Thanks, Molly.''

''Kayla's mother, Molly?'' Sawyer asked. Sophie groped for her purse with the phone and missed. He caught her wrist and tried to direct it into her purse, but she yanked away so harshly that the purse flew from her hand and fell somewhere between her body and the door. She straightened the car out of a dangerous swerve.

''Sorry,'' he said.

''My fault.'' She accepted the blame with a gusty sigh. ''Yes, Kayla's mother, Molly. She's baby-sitting for me tonight.''

The Night Owl's big neon sign of a wide-eyed owl on a tree branch flashed on and off a short distance away. She turned into the half-filled parking lot and braked to a stop near the entrance to the ranch-style building.

The bright lights inside and the sight through the wide windows of people in laughing conversation was warmly inviting, but she didn't seem to notice as she headed for the door, ignoring him. She was a woman on a mission.

"Wait!" he called as she reached for the door handle.

"What?" she asked in surprise.

"I want you to know," he said as he loped the small distance between them and caught the handle himself, "that I'm always a gentleman. Of course, when a woman's trying to outrun me, it's a little more difficult to show good manners." He pulled the door open and swept a hand toward the inside of the restaurant.

She stared at him a moment. He thought she looked a little off balance. That was good. He hated being the only one who didn't understand what was going on.

A sign posted near the register read Seat Yourself, and Sophie didn't hesitate, setting a brisk pace to a high-backed booth at the rear of the restaurant. Watching her march ahead of him in a pair of jeans was even better than the sight of her in her scrubs, he noted. She was small and firm, with just enough fullness to add interest to her movements.

A waitress followed them with menus and a coffeepot. She turned their empty cups over and asked, even as she poured, "Coffee?"

Fortunately, they agreed.

"I'll need cream, please," Sophie said, putting her menu aside.

The waitress promised to be right back.

"Pie with your coffee?" Sawyer asked, perusing the varied menu.

"No, thank you."

"French fries? Cup of soup?"

"No. No."

He closed his menu and put it aside. "You're determined not to enjoy this, aren't you?"

"This is fact sharing," she said politely, "not fun finding."

The waitress returned with cream. Sawyer ordered onion rings with a side of ranch dressing.

As the waitress walked away, Sophie seemed suddenly distracted by his order. "Ranch dressing with onion rings?"

He nodded. "Much better than ketchup. You like onion rings?"

"Love them. But with ketchup."

On sudden inspiration, he waved to the waitress, who was just putting his order on the wheel. She returned to their table. "Could you make that an onion blossom, please?" he asked. "I've just discovered the lady likes onions, too."

"No…" Sophie tried to protest.

But the waitress was already scribbling on her pad. She sent a smiling glance from one to the other. "Romantic," she said dubiously, and left again.

"I don't want…" Sophie began again.

"If you don't like them with ranch," he said, taking the ketchup bottle on the edge of the table and placing it in the middle, "you can put ketchup on them. Or on me. Whatever works."

She stared at him another moment with that look he often got from Killian that said he could not be more foreign if he'd come from another planet. Then she shook her head and folded her arms on the table.

He did the same, to let her know he was ready to listen.

"Okay," she said, looking him in the eye. "You make it impossible to be subtle, so I'll just say it outright."

He waited. He could see that she was trying to decide how best to say whatever it was. She opened her mouth to speak three different times.

He continued to wait.

Tears filled her eyes, then she sniffed, tossed her head and said with startling directness, "I'm frigid."

Chapter Five

Sophie couldn't believe she'd said the words until she heard them herself. And heard them, and heard them. They echoed around her like a yodel in the Alps, an unlikely sound that went on and on. She watched Sawyer Abbott's face for the horror, scorn or pity that should greet such an announcement.

He remained quiet, seemingly unaffected except for a slight frown. "Clinically?" he asked. "I mean, you've seen a doctor?"

"No," she replied. "I just don't want to be with anyone. I'm…I have no desire to ever be…sexual." She experienced a moment of complete disassociation from the situation, marveling, as though she were an observer, at the casual way she was discussing her most intimate sexual secret with a man she barely knew. "I mean, I do, but I'm all…" There was just no explaining it. "Anyway, I don't want to fix it." That was a lie, but it would make all this easier.

"Now, that isn't the truth, is it?" His expression gentled with the question. "You looked me in the eye when you said you were frigid, but you dropped your gaze just now."

That sweetness about him made her want to lean into him, but fighting the impulse was safer. "I don't think it can be fixed," she said, trying to sound dispassionate, unconcerned. "I can't stand to be touched. Emotionally, I want to, but I hate the very thought of…of making love with a man. I'll live to be a lonely but safe old lady all by myself."

When she'd finished that statement, she realized she was looking at the back of a chair placed at an empty table several feet away from them. Not into his eyes. She slid her gaze toward his, to find a slight smile on his lips.

"That was a lie, too, wasn't it?" he asked. "The choosing lonely and safe over happy?"

"No!" she said forcefully, then lowered her voice a decibel. "No. I'm…nervous. I don't usually discuss my sex life with complete strangers."

"I'm not a stranger," he corrected quietly. "I'm The One."

She groaned at him and he laughed lightly. "Okay, Eddie and Emma could be wrong about that, but doesn't whatever's going on here deserve a little effort on our part?"

She faced him with strained patience. She'd wanted to see disgust and then acceptance on his face, followed by his quick retreat. Not this insistence that there was something here that required…effort. She didn't *want* to try. Well, she did, but she knew trying would end in disaster.

"Have you heard anything I've said?" she demanded under her breath. "You're a virile man and I'm a woman who's unable to have sex. Can I put it any plainer than that?"

He leaned closer, his frown deepening. "I heard everything you said," he replied on a scolding note, "and frankly I'm affronted that you'd think sex was the only thing I had on my mind. Give me credit for a little style. There are a lot of things I'd like to know about you, things we might do together. If the day comes that we decide to make love…well, that's a ways down the road."

"I can *never* make love," she insisted quietly. "Touch has become something I can't abide. You'd learn about me, take me places, we'd do all those things together. Then, *a ways down the road—*" she repeated his words with warning emphasis "—you'd be ready and I wouldn't."

He seemed completely unimpressed with the scenario she'd laid out. "You have no way of being sure about that until you take the first step down that road."

"I can tell by the way I feel."

"But you have no idea how I could make you feel."

Before she could counter that, the waitress arrived with their onion blossom. Artfully sliced and opened out like the petals of a giant mum, the onion dipped in batter and deep fried must have been a good eight inches across. The aroma was heavenly; the distraction, very welcome.

"Here you go," the waitress said with that same dubious glance. "I've heard of romances beginning over chocolate cake, but never over an onion."

"We're unique," Sawyer said.

"I'll say." She splashed a little more coffee into their cups and disappeared.

Sawyer spooned a dollop of ranch dressing onto Sophie's plate, then some onto his own.

"Just remove a slice and dip," he directed, demonstrating with a slice of his own. He made a sound of approval.

She reached into the still-hot onion, pulled off a segment, dipped it into the ranch dressing with a reluctant look at him, then took a bite.

For an onion lover, it was ambrosia. The creamy, spicy tang of the dressing was the perfect complement to the sweet and crunchy onion.

"There are no words," she said finally after another bite. "Just what I needed. One more vice."

He arched an eyebrow at her as they dug into the onion together. "Vice?"

"Peanut butter," she confessed, "guacamole, plants for the garden, the Style Channel, socks…"

He rolled his eyes at the innocence of that list. "Some vices."

She sipped her coffee, then laughed. "Well, I can't have sex, so you had to figure they'd be tame."

"Do you want to talk about it?" he asked as she reached for more dressing. He pushed the small bowl toward her.

"No," she said. Then, deciding that wasn't entirely fair, since she'd brought him here to discuss it, she added reluctantly, "Okay. But what is there to say?"

He shrugged. "Well, I'd have thought it was obvious. I was right about the ranch dressing, wasn't I? You were convinced there was nothing in the world like ketchup on an onion ring, and voilà! I've expanded your horizons. How do you know I wouldn't be just as right-on about making love—if and when it happens?''

She stopped eating, put her napkin to her mouth and sat back. "Because I'm sort of...damaged."

He shook his head slowly over that, an expression of gentle indulgence on his face. "You're not damaged. You're a warm and kind woman. You just think every man in the world presents the same threat to you that your husband did."

She sipped more coffee and looked out the window. The whole world inside the restaurant was reflected there. "Don't you want to ask me why I stayed with him?"

"Do you want to tell me?" he asked.

She felt a little desperate. Her voice came out choked and barely audible. "It's hard to explain if you haven't lived with someone who loves you but hurts you, anyway."

"Then I'll just assume you had a good reason," he said.

She would have let the matter go at that, but for the first time since she'd left Bill and hidden out with her children, the facts were putting themselves into order, pushing their way out.

"We had five great years," she said, unable to hold back.

He pushed the onion aside and gave her his full attention.

"We were happy," she went on, her eyes losing focus, "very much in love. Then something changed him." Her gaze shifted back to him and she asked him suddenly, "Did I tell you he was a cop?"

"No."

"He was a cop," she said again. "Vice. Lots of seedy stuff. He was promoted to a squad that was the best, but they'd been at it a long time. I guess they figured they had a few perks coming and helped themselves to a little of the money they found, a few of the women."

He didn't want to hear this, not because it horrified him, but because it upset her. Somehow, without conscious decision on his part, he was getting in deeper than he wanted to go. And yet, he kept going.

She kept talking, so he didn't have time to analyze. Not to touch her in comfort was hard, but that would have hurt her rather than helped, so he folded his arms.

"I didn't know all that then. I just knew he wasn't himself. He was always at work, and when he did come home, he was short-tempered and reclusive. Then one day we had an argument about something stupid...." She shook her head as if, all this time later, it was still hard to believe. "About whether to pitch in with some friends on a gift for a neighbor who was moving away. I thought it was a good idea because the older couple had been kind to our children, but he thought it was an expense we didn't need. I didn't realize then that he was seeing a 911 dispatcher and she was costing him money. Anyway, I offered one more argument after he made what he considered the final decision. And he hit me." She recoiled slightly, as though feeling the slap again.

Sawyer took a sip of coffee, finding it necessary to occupy his hands.

"I was shocked and emotionally hurt, and I thought he was, too. We went for counseling for a year, but it didn't do anything for us. I tried, but nothing changed.'' She seemed to come out of her thoughts to focus on him, as though wanting to make sure he understood what had motivated her. ''You have to understand that for five whole years, there was no sign of the man he was to become. I loved him, believed in him, had his children. I wanted our family to last.'' Then she returned to her thoughts.

''It all began to fall apart again. His outbursts grew more frequent and I filed for divorce, but he told me in no uncertain terms that I had to stay. He had his eye on a promotion and it wouldn't look good to have charges of abuse come out publicly.'' She paused, tears spilling over. ''He threatened to take the children away if I didn't stay. And he had enough legal connections to do it.''

Sawyer didn't know what to say to that, and he couldn't touch her, so he just leaned toward her and said her name. She looked as though she'd have liked to reach for comfort but couldn't.

''I just bided my time,'' she went on finally, sitting back. ''The abuse was sporadic, and he never touched the children, but he wanted sex regularly and all my feeling for him was lost. I endured it by pretending I wasn't there, and now…I hate to be touched. I hate to remember.'' She tossed her head, probably shaking away the thoughts, and let out a ragged sigh. ''Eventually, I met a rape-and-abuse counselor at the hospital where I worked, and she finally helped me get away. Then…Bill died in a chase and I was free at long last.''

She didn't look free. She looked like Houdini shackled in the water tank, trapped and struggling.

"You *are* free," he said softly. "Focus on that. Free to relearn your womanhood. Free to have a full, well-rounded life. Free to find happiness."

She sniffed and directed her attention on him with a wry smile that was more mocking than amused. "Do you *ever* have a negative thought?"

"Sure," he replied. "All the time. Just not about you."

She pulled the onion toward her unconsciously, forked off a bite and dipped it into the dressing. "I don't understand why you'd want to spend time with someone like me, when I hear that dozens of beautiful, less-complicated women are clamoring for your attention. The nurses at the hospital sing your praises because you've done so much for them and for children."

He reached for the onion, relieved to see that she seemed calmer once again.

"Who can explain attraction?" he asked rhetorically. "You feel it for someone or you don't. I'm very attracted to you. If circumstances were different, you'd be attracted to me, too."

"But I've been told by those same nurses that though you're a good human being, you're sort of a love-'em-and-leave-'em kind of guy."

He considered that. "That's not entirely true. I've never been serious enough about anyone to be truly in love."

"At thirty-five?"

"I have important work and a high-maintenance family. Keeps me busy."

She studied him for a long moment with an expression that was hard to read. It felt a little as though she was mentally dissecting him.

"What if I…what if I agreed to see you and you were wrong about my coming out of this? You'd get hurt."

"Life's about taking chances." That was his philosophy in a nutshell. "If you want to be safe all the time, then you don't belong in the game."

"I *do* want to be safe all the time," she said with complete conviction. "I think I have that coming. And I want my children to be safe all the time. Gracie saw Bill hit me the last time, and when she sprang to my defense, he shoved her away and she fell. She's traumatized—"

"Of course she is," he interrupted. "Of course *you* are. But you have to know I'd never hurt you physically. Or your children. I just don't have that in me. And I'd never hurt you emotionally on purpose. I'm rich and spoiled and I have more than anyone should have, but my brothers and I were brought up to love, to work, to care, to value everyone."

She looked into his eyes, her own telling him she could believe that, but she seemed to have a fear or two remaining.

"What?" he asked.

She folded her arms, body language for setting up a barrier, though there was something else in her eyes, that same yearning he'd seen before to lean toward him and accept comfort if only she dared.

"What?" he repeated.

"I'm afraid," she said, "that you're thinking of me as one of your death-defying stunts."

The words stabbed him like a rusty knife.

"That was nasty, Sophie," he accused quietly.

She agreed with a nod but made no apology. "I don't want to be a test of your fearlessness...or your prowess."

He sighed and called for the waitress. "Right now," he said, "you're just a test of my endurance." He asked the waitress to box the leftover onion. "It's great microwaved," he told Sophie.

She smiled tentatively at him. "Great. Tomorrow's breakfast."

As the waitress returned with the check and disappeared to box the onion, Sawyer began to slip out of the booth. Sophie stopped him with a hand on his wrist. He was so surprised that for a moment he couldn't move. He felt every slender fingertip in contact with his flesh.

She snatched her hand away immediately, looking at his arm and then at him as though unable to believe she'd done that.

"Yes?" he asked. He pretended it was nothing, but he knew what a big deal it really was.

She put both hands in her lap. "I'm sorry I said that. It was unfair."

He hated to admit this, but she'd made a great concession, however unconsciously. He could do the same. "Maybe at the very heart of me I don't understand why I love the stunts," he said. "My childhood was complicated, though most of it was wonderful. However, a few bad things happened that have affected me, even though I think I'm dealing with them. But I promise you I'd never use a relationship with you to serve some thrill-seeking need. I like you. I want to know you. It's as simple as that."

She smiled—not a superficial gesture, but emotion felt at something genuinely pleasing.

The waitress returned with the to-go box. "So," she said, "is romance blooming over our onion blossom?"

Sawyer couldn't answer her and turned to Sophie to let her reply.

"We'll be back for the chocolate cake," she said, still smiling.

THE CHILDREN WERE ASLEEP when Sophie got to Molly's just before midnight. "Don't worry about it," Molly said in a low voice as Sophie apologized for keeping her up. "The kids are asleep and Jack and I are just going over the checkbook. He can never balance it without grumbling because I haven't bothered to put in check numbers or something. They're all in sleeping bags in the family room, except Gracie, who's in Kayla's room. Just let them stay the night and I'll take Eddie and Emma to day care with me in the morning." Molly helped out two days a week during the summer in the same day care Sophie used at the Losthampton Presbyterian Church. "Kayla and Gracie have their summer-school art class all day tomorrow."

Sophie felt guilt stricken. Molly was a very busy woman.

"Will you stop it?" Molly insisted as Sophie apologized again. "Tell me how your date was with Sawyer Abbott."

"It wasn't a date," Sophie corrected. "And I didn't want to ask with Sawyer sitting beside me in the car, but how did you know I was with him?"

"Jack ran into the hospital to pick up something he'd left at his office and saw the two of you leave together. Dr. Brown told him Sawyer had taken a tumble and you volunteered to drive him home. When you called to say you were stopping for coffee, I presumed you were with him."

"I was, but it wasn't a date."

"You stopped for coffee. It was a date."

"It was a fact-finding mission."

Molly blinked at her. "Soph, being interested in a man doesn't require military tactics. I mean…" She cleared her throat, looking momentarily uncertain of her ground, then she apparently decided to plunge on. "I know your marriage literally was warfare, but most relationships are peaceful alliances in the interest of a common good."

Sophie fought embarrassment. She had no reason to feel responsible for what had happened to her, but she did, anyway. "Gracie's been talking," she guessed.

"Not to me, to Kayla," Molly said, putting a hand to Sophie's shoulder. "Kayla doesn't tell me everything, but what happened to your family was something she didn't know existed. She shared it with me because she thought it was so wrong. Please don't be upset."

Sophie nodded. "It's all right. I'm not upset. I just hate having to explain it."

Molly shrugged. "I'm not asking you to. Jack comes upon cases of abuse in the hospital more often than you'd believe and I see it occasionally in children at school. I only mentioned this at all because I'm afraid that might have soured you on men. But there are lots of wonderful ones.'' She grinned. ''I've got one, and if I were more open-minded I'd let you borrow him to see for yourself, but I'm selfish. Dating Sawyer, though, would be a good way to learn how great they can be.''

Sophie went home, unable to convince Molly that she hadn't dated Sawyer Abbott. She poured bubble bath under hot running water and climbed in for a soak—a luxury not usually afforded her with the children always needing something.

Could tonight be considered a date? she wondered. All they'd done was share an onion.

And talk about her deepest, darkest secret.

She closed her eyes and groaned, sinking into the suds until they skimmed her chin. The possibility of ever finding a new relationship had always seemed so remote because she'd been sure she simply couldn't do it. She was frozen, her emotions mummified, her feelings tangled and hidden. She couldn't imagine herself ever taking that first step that might lead to something.

Then the truth occurred to her and she sat up, sloshing suds over the side of the tub: *If having coffee with Sawyer Abbott could be considered a date, then she'd taken the first step.*

She'd taken the first step!

A weird little exhilaration bubbled up out of the dark depths of that secret. She'd been mired in the muck of her memories for so long that acknowledging a first step was surprisingly liberating. She was still stuck, but there'd been movement toward change.

Her heartbeat picked up, and she felt a little flicker of hope. And she hadn't had hope in a long, long time.

Chapter Six

Sophie didn't sleep very well, disturbed by alternating bouts of hope and terror. By 5:00 a.m., she wasn't sure which had won. So she busied herself making a breakfast casserole of potatoes, eggs and sausage, which she took over to Molly's at the first sign of light in the kitchen.

Jack, already dressed for the hospital, accepted the large pan from her by the hot pads she held and sniffed. "I have died and gone to heaven," he said feelingly. "But to what do I owe this boon? I'm usually on my own at this hour and stuck with corn flakes."

"You kept my kids last night," she explained as Molly stumbled groggily into the kitchen, red hair on end.

"That's right." Jack carried the casserole to the counter and reached for two plates. "You had that date with Sawyer. Want to join us?"

"It wasn't a date," Molly said on a yawn, wandering blindly toward the casserole. "What is that wonderful aroma? Oh, my. Sophie, will you help us eat this wonderful breakfast?"

"No, thank you," Sophie replied to the invitation as she backed out of the kitchen. "Got to get ready for work."

"Thank you!" Jack called after her.

"My pleasure. And thank you again for taking care of the kids."

By midafternoon she'd dealt with a broken arm, a mild heart attack and stomach pain that proved to be a touchy gall bladder. Then Gary Davidson, one of their regulars, came in looking for painkillers. Today he claimed he was suffering excruciating pain from a kidney stone. According to hospital records, he'd purportedly been passing it for a year and half, as well as suffering from back pain, fibromyalgia and a host of difficult-to-define illnesses. If he didn't get the drugs here, he'd go elsewhere. His method was to trek from hospital to hospital until some doctor who didn't know him prescribed Vicodin or Percocet.

She was happy to turn him over to June Montgomery, the charge nurse who'd already been alerted by another hospital several towns away that he was making the rounds today. Denied at Losthampton Hospital again, he left in a fury.

She was restocking a crash cart when Jack appeared at her side, a memo in his hand. "I need help," he said without preamble.

She looked over her shoulder to the ER floor. She'd been sure it was empty for the moment.

"No, not with patients," he said. "With a fundraising committee function. We want to raise money this year for body huggers for the ER."

She pretended ignorance. "We're going to hire people to hug the patients?"

He smiled flatly. "You're very funny for someone who was delivering breakfast at 6:00 a.m. You know—the plastic blankets with built-in baffles to help hypothermia patients. It's a good idea to be well-stocked in a coastal town filled with ocean-going entertainments."

"Ah. Of course. Sure. What do you need?"

"A replacement for Sandy Gabriel on the committee."

Oh, no. Not membership on a committee. "Jack, I'm not much for meetings. I don't see enough of the kids—"

"That's the beauty of this. It's once a week, but you can take the kids with you if you want. The chairman doesn't mind."

"Who's the chairman?"

"I am."

"Ah. What do I have to do?"

"We're putting the finishing touches on the committee's Annual Fair for Funds." When she looked puzzled, he nodded. "That's right. I keep forgetting you haven't been here long enough to have attended one. We line up the local church and civic groups to sell crafts and food. For a twenty-five-dollar ticket, guests have access to the carnival rides, can sample the food and watch Sawyer's stunt. They have to buy the crafts. The hospital makes a bundle."

"So we have to approach these groups?"

"We've already done that. They're all confirmed, and we've reserved the fairgrounds. All we have to do now is plan the press releases and distribute tickets for sale at various outlets."

The press releases didn't sound like anything she'd

be particularly good at, but she'd happily volunteer for ticket distribution.

"I guess I can do that," she agreed.

"Good," he said. "Next meeting is tonight."

"Here?"

"No. We're meeting at Shepherd's Knoll."

"What?" she demanded. "You mean...Sawyer's home?"

"Yes. He's the other person on the committee. Why? Is that a problem?" Then he seemed to remember about her date/no-date situation with Sawyer Abbott last night. "Ooh," he said. "Puts you in an awkward position? Never mind, I'll ask—"

"No," she said quickly, having to make an instant decision. She'd taken the first step out of her past. And this position on the committee didn't ask any more of her than that she take another step in a different direction—service to the hospital. It would give her the opportunity to meet more people in the community and serve a good cause, and both would be good for her children. "I can do it," she said. "We're not dating, and it isn't awkward."

Well, it might be, but she and Sawyer had parted last night on friendly terms. Certainly he wouldn't have a problem with her being part of the committee.

"Is this event why Sawyer's planning the in-line skating stunt?"

Jack shook his head. "That's for a food bank function. He's being very secretive about what he's doing for us."

She hated to think. "Molly told me he's rappelled off the Abbott Mills building in Manhattan, done sky-boarding, even offered himself on the auction block. Does he have a death wish?''

Jack made a puzzled face. ''Hard to say. He only does these things for charity, but why he's eager to perform such extreme stunts, I couldn't say. Some people like to live on the edge, I guess.''

''And it doesn't bother anyone that he could get killed?''

''He's smart and fit,'' Jack said. ''He knows what he's doing.''

''How can risking one's life when it's not directly to save another's be considered smart?''

''I guess you'll have to ask him.''

She had, as she recalled, but she couldn't recall his answer. She did recollect, though, that she'd felt guilty about accusing him of thinking of her as one of his stunts. And she'd caught his wrist to prevent him from slipping out of their booth before she could apologize.

She remembered the warm, solid feel of his skin; the metal of his watch, also warmed by his skin, against the palm of her hand; the steady pulse under her fingertips, keeping time with the watch. She'd felt his life force—the essence of him.

She'd drawn her hand away quickly, muscle under her touch a hated memory. Then she'd looked into his surprised eyes and seen only interest...kindness.

Jack walked away to take a phone call, and she stood alone in the supply room, wondering if she was making a terrible mistake. What if being near Sawyer made her want to touch him again?

No, she probably wouldn't. Last time had been

a simple impulse, stemming from guilt over what she'd said.

But she was a little worried that she even wanted to put herself in that position. Jack had given her an out. She was worried and exhilarated. She'd taken a step.

She couldn't stop now.

CAMPBELL WALKED INTO the kitchen covered with dust. China followed him in, looking just as disreputable. Her face was smeared with dirt; her hair, tucked under a baseball cap.

"What's going on in the orchard?" Sawyer asked as Kezia puttered over the stove.

"We moved a couple of trees," Campbell replied, "so we can widen the road to make room for the new specialized spray tractor. Got a new environmental spray to use in it that really works!"

"You should see it," China said, her dark eyes alight with enthusiasm. "It has a really low turning radius, reversibility. And air-conditioning! Even Winfield took a spin in it."

Sawyer had a what's-wrong-with-this-picture sort of feeling. Then he realized what it was. "You mean, you two actually agreed on something?" he asked. This was the first time since she'd arrived that he'd seen them in each other's company and not screaming at each other.

"Don't let it get around," China said, hooking a thumb in Campbell's direction. "I'm sure he'll find something that I've done wrong. I'm off to the shower." She headed for the door, then stopped to inspect two movies lying on the edge of the counter.

"*Daddy Day Care* and *Legally Blond II?*" she asked, holding them up. "Your grandkids coming over, Kezia?"

Kezia shook her head and grinned. "They belong to your big brother."

China widened her eyes at Sawyer. "They do?"

"Hospital committee meeting here tonight," he replied. "And one of the members is bringing her children. I thought the kids would be happier in the family room, with the big-screen TV." Once a formal parlor, the large room off the foyer had been turned into a place for relaxing, watching television, listening to music.

China put the movies down and took several steps back toward him. "Her children? Who is she?"

"No one you know," he replied. "Go take your shower." One thing different about having a sister around—even a potential one—was that his brothers had little interest in his love life. China, however, checked out all the women who stopped by to see him. She'd been with them only a few weeks, but with Killian still in Europe with Cordie, and Campbell on her black list, she seemed to enjoy getting to know Sawyer as much as he did her.

"What's her name?" Campbell, apparently bored being at peace with China, was looking for trouble of another sort. He walked up behind Kezia to peer over her shoulder. "Chicken and dumplings!" He grinned at Sawyer. "Your childhood favorite. These kids must be special. So, I guess their mother is, too. Who is she?"

"It's the woman who got him arrested," Kezia put

in casually before he could fend off Campbell and China.

China shrieked and Campbell hooted.

Sawyer rolled his eyes and went to push both of them toward the door. "If you make yourselves presentable," he said, "I might even introduce you over dinner. Now, get out of here so Kezia can focus."

"She can focus no matter what," Campbell disputed. "I want some detail."

"There is none. Go."

China punched Campbell in the arm as they walked out the door. "You didn't tell me he had a girlfriend."

"I didn't know. And keep your mitts off me."

Kezia shook her head over them. "I'm almost grateful those two *weren't* raised together. They might have killed each other."

"I keep hoping they'll find something to like in each other."

"Hope springs eternal. What do you think the children would like for dessert? Cake and ice cream, or apple pie with whipped cream?"

"Cake and apple pie with ice cream and whipped cream," Eddie replied when asked the question several hours later. He'd eaten two helpings of chicken and dumplings.

Emma had talked through dinner instead of eating, but now seconded Eddie's approach to dessert.

"That's a little greedy," Sophie corrected gently. "Pick one."

"What about one now," China suggested, "and one after the meeting?"

"That way, China gets to try both," Campbell said

with a knowing glance at her. She sent him a threatening look.

"Can I have Gracie's?" Eddie asked. "She didn't want to come."

"Gracie had made plans with a friend," Sophie put in quickly, apparently hoping to cover Eddie's revelation. "She's ten, and her best friend lives right across the road."

"Kayla Spoonby," Sawyer explained to Campbell.

"Ah," he said. Then he added for China's benefit, "Longtime friends of the family. Kayla's father, Jack, is administrator of the hospital."

Sawyer thought it odd that Campbell thwarted China at every turn, but offered the courtesy of keeping her involved in the conversation when it became too inside. But then, Campbell confused him all the time.

"Speaking of Jack," Sawyer said, "where is he, anyway? He said he wouldn't make it for dinner, but he hoped to make it for dessert. He loves Kezia's apple pie."

"Can I have his if he doesn't come?" Eddie asked.

As though on cue, the telephone rang. It was Jack, who explained to Sawyer that the meeting that had kept him from joining them for dinner was still going on and he couldn't leave. "Call me tomorrow," he said, "and tell me what you want me to do. The *Leader's* publisher owes me a favor. I got his daughter a job in Medical Records."

Sawyer agreed to do that, wondering if this was Jack's way of helping him with Sophie, or if he genuinely was busy. True, Sawyer had asked Jack to ask Sophie, without mentioning his name, if she'd serve on the committee. But he hadn't expected Jack to go this far—if he was.

After dessert, Sawyer got the children set up in the parlor with one of their movies. Emma went immediately to Versace, curled up in a big chair, and stroked him. The cat looked tense but didn't move. Then he began to purr. Sawyer was amazed, though still reluctant to leave the unpredictable cat with the children.

"Don't worry about the cat," Winfield said, appearing behind him. "I'll keep an eye on him and the children."

"Thank you, Winfield."

Back in his office, Sawyer told Sophie that Jack wasn't coming.

As he'd anticipated, she eyed him suspiciously.

"Before you let that thought form," he said, putting his event notes on the small table between two large chairs in his office upstairs, "I want you to remember how you hated yourself after accusing me of things I'm not guilty of."

She pursed her lips at him. "Are you sure you didn't put him up to this?"

"I am not responsible," he said, careful not to lie, "for his meeting running late. I don't control the Community Action board."

She studied him a moment, probably trying to decide if he was being honest or not. He met her gaze intrepidly.

"All right," she said, taking one of the chairs. "You'll have to catch me up on all this, I'm afraid. I hadn't moved to Losthampton yet when the event

took place last year. I don't know much about it.''
Then she looked him in the eyes. "But I am on to
you, so watch it.''

SOPHIE WAS A LITTLE intimidated by her surround-
ings. Sawyer said his father had called the difficult-
to-define architectural style of the house Seaside Vic-
torian. The structure had three levels, with a tower,
porches all around, large, long windows and a mag-
nificent view of the ocean from the top floor. The
whole was painted a cheery butter yellow.

Inside, everything was bright and cozy, despite the
large dimensions of the rooms. Everything was spot-
less yet still inviting.

Sawyer was patient and thorough in explaining the
event in detail and answering all her questions. He
then laid out the committee's remaining duties and
asked her to pick what she was most comfortable doing.

"I don't think I could do press releases," she said,
"but I am efficient with tedious tasks. I can distribute
the tickets, keep track of them, then collect them the
morning of the event. I suppose we'll also be selling
them at the entrance?''

He nodded. "We usually presell about half, then
there's a big crowd buying at the entrance. We've had
great food in the past and the event gains momentum
every year. If I make flyers to put up on storefronts
and in public places, can you get them around?''

"Sure," she agreed. "The kids'll like helping with
that. What about staffing the day of the event?''

"The committee does that along with volunteers
from hospital staff."

She gulped. "Three of us?"

"Actually, there are ten people on the committee." He laughed at her panic. "But they've already done their jobs. They've lined up the restaurants, solicited contributions toward the advertising and collected door prizes. Now it's up to us to make sure everything else comes together. But we'll all gather that night."

"Minus you," she said, sitting back in her comfy velvet chair to enjoy the sight of him relaxed in beige cotton slacks and a soft green polo shirt. She'd managed to pull off a professional distance, she thought, while discussing the event with him, but all the while he talked and leaned close to show her old flyers and previous press releases, always careful not to touch her, she found herself wanting to touch him. But she didn't. "I presume you'll be performing some kind of stunt?"

"I will," he confirmed. "We're keeping the nature of it under wraps, though."

"Is that so no one tries to stop you?"

"No one *could* stop me."

"What if your mother asked you not to do it?"

He shook his head. "She wouldn't. I've done seven or eight already, and she's never asked me not to." He put down the pen with which he'd been taking notes and looked at her with a suddenly personal intensity. "Are you worried enough about me to ask me not to do it?"

"No," she denied. "But I am worried about *why* you do it."

"I told you. I do it for charity."

"Yes." She added her notes to the information folder he'd given her, closed it and placed her purse on top of it. "I'd better take the children home."

"But China promised them a second dessert."

"It's almost eleven and I have to be up at six in the morning." She had to get out of there. She was beginning to imagine all the places her fingertips could go—his cheek, his chin, his hair, his shoulder. She hadn't extricated herself from her quagmire enough to even think below the pectorals, but this far was dangerous enough. If he touched her in return, she'd freak. She knew she would.

He led the way to the kitchen, intending to pack up desserts to go, only to find that Kezia had already done so and left him a note on the refrigerator. So he went to the family room. There Eddie held the remote, bleary-eyed, Emma was asleep with Hermione, and Versace lay atop the throw with which Winfield had covered her.

"But I'm not done, Mom," Eddie complained when Sophie had to help him stand up.

"You can take the movie home with you," Sawyer said, ejecting it, putting it back in the sleeve and handing it to him. "And Kezia has your dessert all packed up."

"But I wanted to eat it here!" he grumped sleepily.

"Your mom has to get up early in the morning," Sawyer explained. "So you have to cooperate. But you can come back anytime you want."

"Okay."

Had Sophie tried to explain, she'd have gotten an endless litany of complaints. She gave Sawyer a grudging smile for sparing her that.

Winfield removed Versace, who yowled a complaint and ran off. Sawyer scooped Emma and Hermione into his arms and followed Sophie as she led

Eddie through the kitchen to collect the desserts. Eddie insisted on carrying them. Apparently seeing the potential danger there, Sawyer put them in a small picnic basket he retrieved from the top of the refrigerator.

"My mother uses it when she goes to the beach," he said, handing it to Eddie.

Eddie's tired eyes widened in surprise. "You have a mother?"

"Sure," Sawyer replied. "Everybody has a mother."

"But you're a grown-up."

"Yes. When *you're* a grown-up you'll still have your mother. Mine's my stepmother."

"What does that mean?"

"Ah…my first mother went away, so my father got married again and that lady became my stepmother."

"Do you like her?"

"Very much."

"Not everybody's got a father, though," Eddie said. He liked his details in order. Sophie could almost predict what was coming. "Me and Gracie and Emma don't."

"Yes, I know."

"Do you have one?"

"I did, but he died."

"Can't you get a step one like your mother?"

Emma began to stir in Sawyer's arms, so Sophie put an end to the conversation.

"You can ask more question another time, Eddie," she said, pushing him gently toward the door. "Right now we have to get home. Mr. Abbott needs to get to bed, too."

"Next time we could make him dinner," Eddie proposed, walking out into the floodlit. front of the house, where she'd left her car. Sawyer had offered to send his chauffeur for her, but she couldn't imagine riding in the back of a limousine. Eddie added, "But we don't cook as good as Kezia."

Sophie's feelings would have been hurt if that hadn't been so true. She opened the back door of her car and took the hamper from Eddie so that he could scramble in and buckle his seat belt.

Sawyer sat Emma up in her seat and held her slumping body up so that Sophie could buckle her belt. Their hands touched inadvertently several times.

In each case, she'd tried to concentrate on not pulling away, but then he did, apparently sure she'd want him to. She experienced an odd coursing of energy each time, heat running under her skin where it had connected with his. Emma finally secured, Sophie closed the back door and turned to face Sawyer.

"Kezia got away before I could tell her how much we all enjoyed dinner," she said. "Please thank her for me. And for the extra dessert."

"She's always loved her work and does it with great style. She'll be happy you appreciate it."

He stayed a small distance away from her, sensitive to her proximity issues, she was sure. But she wished he were a little closer. She kept wanting to lean, to touch, but she couldn't extend herself too far.

She offered her hand, realizing even as she did so what a big step this was for her. A man's hand had become a very dangerous thing to her the last few years of her marriage.

Another step! she thought in silent amazement.

Sawyer studied her outstretched hand dubiously. "You sure?" he asked. "The thank-you was enough."

"I'm sure," she said. "This is…something else."

He wrapped his hand gently around hers, held it for a moment, his grasp warm and strong—and had he held her any longer, the strength in it might have overriden her momentary courage, but he tightened his hold just a little, then freed her.

A sigh ran through her, and it wasn't just relief.

"That was brave," he praised.

"It's easy for other people," she said with a shrug, thinking what an odd conversation this was to have at almost midnight while standing next to a car with two sleepy children inside. It was bigger than the words they exchanged. "Have you noticed how many people hug when they meet? Male and female friends hug all the time. I'm just learning to shake hands."

He smiled. "Oh, one day you'll spot me walking in your direction and you'll come running to me and throw your arms around me without giving it a second thought."

"You think so?"

"I do. I'd even bet on it."

She demurred politely. "I'm sorry. I'm not a gambler."

"True," he said, opening the driver's door. "You've earned the right to be safe, and gambling often isn't. But you just offered me your hand. That was, in effect, a bet that I wouldn't hurt you."

"You promised you wouldn't," she said, slipping in behind the wheel. "I thought that made it a sure thing."

"Provided you trust me."

"I do."

His smile widened. "Then, we're getting someplace."

That might be true, but she was too heady with the enormity of her success to deal in specifics. "I'm getting home. Thank you again."

"Sure. I'll call you when the tickets are printed. And I'll bring the flyers by the hospital when they're ready. Bye, Eddie!"

"Bye, Sawyer!"

Sophie drove home, euphoric. She'd behaved almost like a normal person. She couldn't quite believe it. She'd visited a private home for dinner; she'd shaken Sawyer's hand.

Was there actually hope for her after all?

SAWYER WAS BUSY for several days with other members of the foundation board, reviewing grant applications, then taking time to practice his motorcycle stunt for the hospital benefit. He'd gotten the idea while channel-surfing late one night and coming upon a documentary about motorcycle stuntmen in which one of them rode through a ring of fire.

It occurred to him that he could do that. He'd ridden in his youth, and he felt sure it wouldn't take long to regain his "seat." Jumping the bike through fire would be a little over the top, but that was what sold tickets.

He could have made time to see Sophie, but he thought it would be wise to lie low for a while, do nothing that she might interpret as applying pressure. He still couldn't quite believe she'd shaken his hand.

He knew that had to have been hard for her, but she'd wanted to do it, and that was the most promising thing of all.

He immersed himself in work, gave away a lot of money, arbitrated quarrels between Campbell and China. They disagreed on the new sign intended for the vine-covered arch over the entrance to the property.

"You've been here—what?" Campbell asked of China as they looked over sketches the sign maker had brought. They were in Campbell's office, a cluttered, sun-filled room near the kitchen. "Three weeks? You don't even get to offer an opinion."

"Anyone can offer an opinion," China argued. "It's America. Unless of course Shepherd's Knoll has seceded. And why are you afraid of my input, anyway? It's not as though I expect you to listen to it."

"It's because you have input on *every*thing," Campbell growled at her. "Nobody's sure what your position is yet, and you're swaggering around here like the eldest *son!*"

"You know what this is about?" China turned to Sawyer, who listened from the doorway. "He's angry because I'm better on the new tractor than he is. I can turn tighter than he can. Well, as much as I like thinking I might belong here, I hate the thought of being part of anything that involves him!" She pointed an accusatory finger at Campbell and marched away.

"Good going," Sawyer said to Campbell. "You just made a young woman with no family feel unwelcome here, where she hoped to belong."

Campbell scoffed. "I can't help it. I don't like her."

"Why? Are you afraid there're now too many ways for the famous Abbott fortune to go?"

Fury leaped into Campbell's eyes. Sawyer had to give him credit. A couple of years ago Campbell would have punched Sawyer for that.

"That's not it and you know it," Campbell finally replied darkly.

"Then what *is* it? Guilt, because if she is Abby, the last thing you did before she disappeared was close your door in her face? Are you really mad at yourself, but find it easier to take your feelings of guilt out on her?"

"You don't know anything about it." Campbell angrily placed a weight on the drawings and stomped to the doorway, expecting Sawyer to move out of the way.

Sawyer held his ground. "Go ahead and explain it to me."

"Get out of my way."

"I'd just like a little respite from your constant snarling. The whole household would."

"Well, you can all relax. I'm leaving."

He was always talking about leaving. Then Sawyer remembered the important message he'd been waiting for, the one he'd accused China of losing. He must have found it.

"You got the job?" Sawyer asked.

Campbell, squared his shoulders. "No, I didn't." His tone was aggressive. "But I'm going on another interview."

"Where?"

"None of your business. I don't want you to visit me if I get the job."

Sawyer looked into his brother's eyes and tried to think back to what could have caused his hostility. Sawyer and Killian had teased him when they were children, but how many little brothers in the world who could make the same claim had grown up to feel secure, anyway?

"If you're determined to leave," Sawyer said, stepping out of his way, "would you please stop making China's life miserable so she can learn the job and we aren't left without a competent estate manager?"

"Anybody can do my job."

"You make it sound as though she couldn't possibly."

Campbell opened his mouth to respond, then changed his mind and stormed past him, through the kitchen and out the door. It slammed with a reverberating crash.

Sawyer always felt like a failure after his confrontations with Campbell, but he doubted that even the diplomatic Killian could have led that conversation to a peaceful conclusion.

The telephone rang. Sawyer knew that Kezia had ridden into town with Daniel, and picked it up.

"Sawyer?" It was Chloe's voice. "It's me. Your wicked stepmother."

"*Maman,*" he said, trying to cheer his tone. "How are you? How's Tante Bijou?"

"Tante Bijou has taken a significant turn for the better," she said. "Just this morning we had tea and brioches in the garden, and I talked to her about coming home with me when she is feeling stronger. Her house is wonderful, but the staff can't bully her the way I do, so I think I'll bring her home with me for the rest of the summer.''

"Is she willing to come?"

"Yes. She thinks it would be wonderful to see her great-nephews. I trust that's true? That the three of you haven't started a war and split up our holdings like some family in a medieval saga?"

He hesitated before answering, marveling at the thread of truth in her words, considering Campbell's determination to leave.

"Non!" she exclaimed, sounding horrified. "You have not had a falling-out! There is always trouble when Killian isn't there to keep the peace."

"Relax, Mom," he said quickly. "Nothing's wrong. Campbell and I just had a few words, that's all."

"About what?"

"You know how he's always looking for work elsewhere."

"Oh, that!" She sounded relieved. He'd keep the news about Brian and China to himself. Wait until she heard there were now five of them in the Bermuda Triangle of peacekeeping. "Is Campbell in?"

"He just took off. Want me to see if I can find him?"

"No. Just tell him I said that I'll be expecting calm and quiet when I come home with Tante Bijou." She was silent for a moment, then she asked tauntingly, "Guess who I saw two days ago?"

"De Gaulle?" he guessed jokingly.

"De Gaulle is dead, *chou.*"

"Brigitte Bardot?"

"Sawyer! Killian and Cordie. They were on their

way to London to stay for a while before flying home.''

''To stay for how long?''

''Until they get bored.''

Sawyer groaned. ''Killian's never bored. He's even fascinated by the stock market reports.''

She sighed wistfully. ''They were having such a wonderful time. I was so happy to see that. Now, when will you find a woman who makes you happy?''

''I've always been happy.''

''How many stunts do you have lined up?''

He hesitated, sure the question was a setup to prove him wrong. ''Only two,'' he replied finally.

''Then you are not happy. You wish to die.''

''I don't wish to die!'' he said forcefully. Why did everyone think that? ''My stunts are for charity.''

''That's what you tell everyone, but we know better.''

He could see no end to a conversation in this direction. ''I'm happy Tante Bijou is improved. Tell her we look forward to seeing her. Frankly, I'll be so happy when you and Killian and Cordie finally do get home and I can stop riding herd on this crowd.''

''This crowd?'' she asked in surprise. ''Who is there besides Campbell?''

He could have bitten his tongue. ''Well...you know, Kezia always needs a lot of attention. And Winfield would frisk the mailman if I didn't keep an eye on him.''

She laughed—fortunately.

''I'll be home soon,'' she promised. ''Two weeks, maybe three.''

"Good. We'll look forward to that. Bye, Mom. I love you."

"I love you, too, *cher*. And please give Campbell my love."

"I will," he promised.

He delivered the message over dinner. China, bless her, appeared at the table in a cheerful mood, as though the argument between her and Campbell hadn't even happened. She wore a white cotton dress that spoke of summer and innocence.

Though twenty-six, she did have a sweetness about her that seemed to fit that ingenue image.

"I'm sorry I couldn't tell her about you," he said.

She dismissed his words with a wave of her salad fork. "Please stop apologizing for the fact that we have to wait. The last thing I'd want to do is hurt the woman I've longed to meet all these years. And it should happen face-to-face. Meanwhile, it's generous of you to allow me to stay."

Her gracious reply made even Campbell look repentant. "I'm sorry about earlier," he said. "I was having a bad day."

She studied him. "You do understand that I don't want anything out of this meeting except the meeting. And I particularly don't want anything that's yours. If your mother *is* my mother, then you're my brother and I wouldn't want to start a relationship by skating your money or your stuff."

Campbell closed his eyes for a moment. "It isn't about money. And don't ask me what it is about."

China nodded again and went back to her salad, sending a shrug in Sawyer's direction. "The best part about discussing anything with Campbell is that he's the only one who gets to talk."

Chapter Seven

Sophie hadn't heard from Sawyer in four days. It amazed her that she could count the time to four days, twenty-three hours and—she consulted the ER clock—seventeen minutes.

She should be happy about that. In fact, she had no idea why she wasn't. She'd done nothing to encourage him and everything to discourage him. A handshake, though a very big deal to her, had probably been nothing at all to him.

Yet he'd said it had been brave of her, so he must have known it was.

She tried to stop thinking about him as she went to the lockers to change her clothes and get her purse. But her brain simply approached Sawyer from a different direction.

Odd that a woman battling frigidity was wondering why the man she'd tried so hard to put off was finally...put off. Maybe he'd thought things through and decided she was right. The world—or at least, Long Island—was probably filled with women who had no such issues and would be happy to have him touch them and make love to them.

Why would he risk dealing with a woman who had to brace herself to shake hands?

Because he was a risk taker. A gambler. He'd said so himself.

She slammed her locker door and made herself think about dinner instead of Sawyer. Changed into black overalls over a yellow T-shirt, she went through the ER to check next week's schedule. Since Sandy Gabriel would be out for several weeks with her broken leg, Sophie might have to work a few more swing shifts. In which case she should consider hiring a baby-sitter rather than leaving her children with Molly when she worked evenings. Though they'd often teased each other about feeling like a couple of mother cats, raising each other's kittens, Molly did have a husband who had a right to her attention.

I, Sophie mused, facing reality as she looked for her name in the shift assignments, *have no one waiting for my attention.*

Happy to see no surprises on the schedule, she headed toward the door but stopped at the sounds of a commotion at the other end of the room. She turned to see Gary Davidson, the drug seeker, shouting at the charge nurse. She'd probably refused his request for Percocet again.

He was dirty and desperate-looking, and grew more agitated when June spoke to him again. Sophie couldn't hear their conversation but presumed that the experienced nurse had simply held firm. Which would just send him to try the next hospital, but he'd probably worked his way up and down the island already.

Sophie was trying to decide whether to call Security, when Jack came out of his office to investigate the noise. The nurse apparently explained the problem and Jack exchanged words with Davidson, who seemed to be appeased. He started toward the front doors, but when Jack disappeared into his office, he suddenly changed direction, overturned the crash cart Sophie had recently restocked and ran straight for her, wild-eyed.

Molly would take care of her children, she thought with a curious detachment as he reached for her. Gracie would be happy as long as she was with Kayla, and Eddie and Emma would always find their own happiness.

Even as Davidson grabbed her arm and twisted it behind her, she felt more disappointment than panic. She'd seen violence coming at her enough times toward the end of her marriage that she didn't feel the terror and surprise most people did under attack, only a grim sense of not being safe after all, even though Bill was gone.

No, damn it! she told herself as Davidson caught her throat in the crook of his arm. She was sick and tired of being manhandled, sick and tired of being shouted at, sick and tired—

Her anger was snuffed instantly when he grabbed her bare upper arm and held her to him. His fingers felt as though they were pressing into her bones, and her brain suddenly became a kaleidoscope of horrible memories—slaps, shoves, lovemaking she wanted no part of. Hands pushing her, hands holding her down, hands stroking her until her soul oozed out of her pores to escape the moment.

SAWYER WALKED IN THE BACK door of the ER, wondering if Sophie had left yet. He'd brought the flyers for the hospital event, and hoped he could talk her into having coffee to discuss where to post them. It wasn't necessary, of course; he was sure she could figure that out. But he was getting impatient with his plan to give her space. He'd expected it to lend him perspective, help him assess the ever-growing seriousness of his feelings for her. Instead, it just made him impatient to see her again.

He was so preoccupied with the thought that he didn't realize there was a problem until he was almost on it. A man with his back to him was screaming about someone getting him Percocet now or he would break the woman's neck.

Jack stood a small distance away, speaking calmly, though he looked anything but, and an older nurse stood beside him, clearly terrified.

"Let her go," Jack was saying, "and we'll talk about the Percocet."

Only then did Sawyer notice the stream of dark hair over the man's shoulder. It belonged to a woman bent backward and held captive in the guy's arms. Then he saw a pair of beige slip-ons. He recognized them as Sophie's and finally understood what was going on. The man had her in a stranglehold with one arm while the other held her immobile. Any woman would be terrified, but he could only imagine what it was doing to her.

The man had no weapon that Sawyer could see, at least from the back, and his hands were occupied with Sophie. Without considering other options, Sawyer walked around the front of the man, enjoyed his startled expression for one brief second, then punched him in the face. He yanked Sophie toward him as the man sank like a stone.

The moment after he drew Sophie free, Sawyer let her go, not sure if comfort in the form of touch would be welcome even now. Jack and the nurse came to her. The nurse pushed her onto a stool, checked the already developing bruises on her throat and asked her if she could breathe.

Sophie strained a little for air, her eyes wide and tortured. But she nodded quickly. "Yeah," she said in a strained voice. "I'm okay." Sawyer would have been happy to hit the man again, though he hadn't regained consciousness yet.

The nurse gave Sophie a cup of water while Jack called the police.

Sophie met Sawyer's eyes as she handed back the cup, a thank-you in them, and something else—a kind of pleading he couldn't identify precisely but figured he didn't have to. He went to her and offered his hand, palm up.

"I don't know whether or not to touch you," he said softly as Jack spoke on the phone and the nurse leaned over the attacker's inert body, "but if you need something solid to hold on to, you can touch me."

At most, he'd thought she might take his hand. When she stood and threw her arms around him, he was surprised into stillness. Did he close his arms around her or not?

As she trembled against him, he finally did envelop her, thinking she could always pull away if she wanted to. But she didn't.

Jack, still on the phone, pointed him to his office.

Sawyer held Sophie to his side and led her into the small, tidy room where Jack conducted hospital business. He tried to put her in a chair, but she refused to loosen her grip on him.

"Just let me hold on to you," she pleaded softly.

"Okay." He tightened his hold just a little, and she tightened hers. She wasn't crying, but she'd leaned her forehead against his shoulder and seemed to concentrate on drawing in air.

"I'm so sorry that happened," he said, putting a hand to her hair. He half expected her to draw away, but she put her cheek to his shoulder, instead, facing away from him.

"I'm glad you were there," she replied. "I was just about to lose it, when I saw your face."

"Are you sure you're okay?"

She raised her head from his shoulder and sighed. "Yes. I feel scared again, and I hate that, but I'm okay."

"Hey. That wasn't someone who lives in your home and can come after you day after day. That was someone we're going to file charges against, put away, then see that he gets help. He's not going to bother you again."

She nodded and drew another breath, looking steadier this time. "Okay. I like that idea."

"And I don't know if you've noticed or not, but you have a death grip on me."

She smiled wryly. "I have noticed."

She was forced to relinquish her hold when the police arrived and asked her questions. Jack placed a chair for Sawyer beside Sophie, and though Sawyer didn't touch her, she appeared to take comfort in his nearness. He told her he'd called Molly to explain what had happened, and to tell her Sophie would be late picking up the children.

The older nurse described Sawyer's part in things in dramatic detail. "Of course, he's the one who does all those stunts for charity," she said, "so I guess we shouldn't be surprised that he turns out to be a real hero."

"The guy wasn't armed," Sawyer reminded everyone. "And I had a couple of inches on him. It wasn't that heroic."

"You probably saved Sophie's life!" she insisted.

He turned to Sophie, sure she was remembering her accusation that he might be considering a relationship with her as just another of his stunts. But she appeared more amused by his discomfort than upset by June's observation.

"I was very glad to see him," Sophie said. "Thank you, Sawyer."

"My pleasure, Sophie," he replied.

Then she frowned and asked, "What were you doing here, anyway?"

"I came to deliver the flyers you were going to post for us." He grinned. "But I'm not sure what I did with them. They're probably all over the ER floor."

"They're in a tidy pile on my desk," June said. "They were all over the floor, but I picked them up."

By the time Sophie and Sawyer were finally able to leave it was after six.

"I guess the grateful thing for me to do," she said as they walked side by side across the parking lot, "would be to invite you to dinner."

He stopped beside her car to look down at her.

"You don't have to be grateful." They were back to not touching and he hated that, but he did have the memory of those few minutes. "I do like it, though, when you say you were glad to see me."

She elbowed him shyly—not exactly a touch, but it would do. "I really was. I was…" Her brow furrowed. "His hands on me reminded me—"

"It's over," he interrupted. "We don't have to talk about it."

"I do," she insisted. "I have to tell you what it meant to me to see you standing there like the wrath of God. I couldn't believe it. I was sure my neck would break, and I'd been wondering about what would happen to my children—"

"Please stop." He raised his hand to put a finger to her lips, then changed his mind. "Your neck is beautiful and your children are waiting at this very moment for you to come home. You can have me over for dinner when you're feeling less…"

She challenged him with a smile. "Less what?"

"Less upset."

"I got over being upset when you held me."

That surprised him, but he didn't want her to feel she owed him anything—touch in particular—because of what happened.

"Less frightened, then."

"I got over being frightened when you held me."

"Sophie…"

"You're afraid I feel indebted, aren't you?"

He had to appreciate a woman who didn't tiptoe around an issue. "Yes, I am."

She opened her door, tossed her purse inside, then folded her arms and looked into his face. "Well, of course I feel indebted. But that doesn't mean I'm going to ravage you out of gratitude.''

"It doesn't?" he asked in feigned disappointment. Or maybe it wasn't feigned.

She slapped his arm. "Of course it doesn't. But I would like to thank you with dinner. Mind you, 'We don't cook as well as Kezia,'" she said, mimicking Eddie's review of the other night. "But if you like spaghetti, it's one of the kids' favorites and they'll be thrilled to have you at the table.''

"What time?" he asked.

She checked her watch. "Want to just come out with me? You can lend a hand, and I'll drive you back to your car afterward.''

"Gracie won't like it," he warned her as he walked around to the passenger's side.

"She just has to see a different kind of man. I think her spending so much time with Kayla's family helps, but Jack works so hard he isn't often there. Kayla sure talks him up, though."

Sawyer nodded. "He's a great guy."

Gracie was not at all pleased when she and Kayla ran out to greet her mother's car and found that Sawyer had accompanied Sophie home. Kayla, however, made up for her friend's lack of enthusiasm. She took his hand and pulled him toward the house while Sophie ran across the road to pick up Eddie and Emma.

"Make yourself at home!" Sophie shouted as she hurried off. "Gracie, pour him a pop!"

Jack had apparently told Molly what had happened, and she in turn had told Kayla, who was a little of a drama queen to begin with.

"It's like a Sandra Bullock movie!" she exclaimed

as she sat beside him on a blue-and-yellow flowered sofa in a room filled with eclectic odds and ends that came together as comfortable and cozy. Sophie's warmth, considering what she'd been through, always surprised him. "You saved Sophie's life! You *have* to get married."

"No, they don't!" Gracie returned from the kitchen with a tall glass filled to the brim with cola.

Sawyer accepted it from her with a polite thank-you.

"You have to use a coaster," she said, taking one from a small stack near a pot of flowers and slapping it on the table. "Just because we don't have a fortune doesn't mean we can't take care of our things."

She'd said it, but it sounded very much as though she was repeating her mother.

"I understand," he said, placing the glass on the coaster.

"My mom's never getting married again," she went on, frowning at him from a chair on the other side of the coffee table. "She's been hurt enough."

"Gracie, he saved her life!" Kayla said, her hands over her heart. "Like a prince or...or a bodyguard! He protected her! The other man was going to kill her!"

Gracie's face crumpled, her very adult hostility suddenly dissolving into very childlike tears.

Sawyer panicked. A woman's tears were one thing, but he didn't know what to do about a young girl's.

"She's fine," he tried to reassure her. "The man didn't have a gun or anything. He was just confused and angry."

"And he used her as a hostage to get drugs!"

Kayla contributed, as if she were Sandra Bullock's overeager script girl.

Gracie cried harder. "Kayla, hush, please." Sawyer got up and walked around the table. "Gracie, he didn't have time to hurt her. She's fine."

"My dad hurt her a lot," she wept. She was curled up in the corner of a big chair, her knees drawn up, her eyes miserable.

"I know he did. But I would never do that."

"She never told me he hurt her. He yelled a lot, but I didn't know he hurt her."

He sat on the hassock in front of the chair. "She probably didn't want you to worry."

"Then I saw him do it, and when I went to help her, he pushed me."

"She told me about that."

"He said he was sorry, but sorry doesn't fix everything."

Another quote, he guessed.

"Mom's lip was bleeding and there was a cut over her eye." Gracie gave him a suddenly venomous look. "He talked nice to me and said he loved us, but then he hurt Mom."

"I wouldn't do that."

"*He* told me he wouldn't do that, but I saw it!"

"Not everybody hits, Gracie," he said, wanting to get that through to her not only for his chances with this family, but for her peace of mind. "Some people just talk when they have problems, and they never hurt anybody else."

She looked into his eyes, hers dark puddles of doubt. "But how do you know who's who?"

A simple but pointed question.

The front door burst open, and Eddie came through. He launched himself at Sawyer like a rocket. Emma piled on top of them and Gracie ran off, the sound of a sob in her wake. Kayla followed her.

"What happened?" Sophie asked worriedly, staring after them.

"Kayla was a little dramatic about what happened this morning, and Gracie got upset." He shifted Eddie onto one knee while Emma climbed onto the other. "I'm sorry. Then she started talking about her dad and…"

Sophie nodded. "Okay. Eddie, you and Emma are in charge of setting the table. I'm sure Sawyer will help you if you'll tell him where things are. Okay?" she asked Sawyer quietly.

"Of course. Come on, guys. Show me what to do."

Sophie disappeared down a corridor as Emma importantly explained where to find the silverware.

SOPHIE DISCOVERED GRACIE SITTING in the middle of her glow-in-the-dark stars bedspread, sobbing while Kayla held an arm around her shoulders.

"She's afraid she'll be all alone if you die," Kayla announced. "Because of your death scare today. And even though Sawyer seems nice, she's afraid he'll turn out to be like her dad. That's a lot to worry about."

Sophie was sometimes grateful for Kayla's precocious but insightful observations. She herself would have needed the better part of an hour to get that out of Gracie.

"Kayla, would you mind taking the French bread

from the freezer and softening a cube of butter for me. You've done that for me before.''

Kayla nodded. "Right. A couple of seconds in the microwave. Then I have to go home. Mom says I can't stay for dinner tonight so you can have some private time with Sawyer.'' As she went off to do as Sophie asked, Sophie sat beside Gracie.

"I'm sorry you were frightened, sweetie,'' she said, putting an arm around her. "I was scared, too, for a minute. Then Sawyer came along and took care of everything.''

Gracie nodded, swiping away tears with the heel of her hand. "That's what Molly told me. I don't want you to die, Mom.''

"Of course you don't. I don't, either.'' Sophie knew that a very personal issue underlay Gracie's concern for her. "But if that was to happen before you were grown up, I have it all worked out. You'd all go live with Kayla's family.''

Gracie considered that, then turned to Sophie with a grimace. "I love them and everything, but I still don't want anything to happen to you.''

Sophie nodded. "I promise to do my best not to let anything happen to me.''

"Okay.'' Gracie continued to frown. "Are you gonna marry Sawyer?''

"No,'' she denied quickly. "Why?''

"Kayla said you had to get married. That it was like a Sandra Bullock movie.''

"Sandra Bullock movies are fun, but they're fiction.''

"Not real, right?''

"Right. I like Sawyer, though, and I'd like it if he spent some time with us."

Gracie expelled a disgruntled sigh. "I don't like him."

"Why?"

"I just don't."

"He isn't Daddy, Gracie," Sophie said gently, pulling her into her shoulder. "I know Daddy shocked and disappointed you, and that's a tough thing to happen to a little girl. But you can't let that make you afraid of all men. Some of them are very nice."

Gracie put her hands over her face and started to cry again.

"Honey, what's the matter? Are you afraid Sawyer will hurt you? 'Cause I promise you he wouldn't."

Gracie shrugged. "That's what he said."

"Is that it? You know you can tell me anything."

Gracie nodded, but said no more. Sophie accepted that she would have to be patient and wait until Gracie was ready to share the problem, whatever it was.

"Will you make a salad for me while I fix spaghetti?"

Gracie slid off her bed. "Does he have to have dinner here all the time because he saved your life?"

"Not all the time," Sophie answered, "but once in a while. I'll bet you'll learn to like him."

"What if I don't want to?"

"A lot of times we turn out to be wrong about things we're very sure about."

Gracie nodded. "Like Daddy."

That hadn't been Sophie's point, but she found it hard to call Gracie wrong on her interpretation.

Chapter Eight

"This is my soldier collecshun…" Eddie opened what looked like an old 5¼ diskette box filled with green plastic soldiers. Sawyer was on a privately conducted tour of Eddie's and Emma's bedrooms. "My dinosaur collecshun…" He shook out the contents of an old oatmeal drum on which someone had pasted stickers of dinosaurs. The farm-theme bedspread was covered with plastic prehistoric animals in bright colors. Emma hung over them, pointing out different species. Eddie yelled at her not to touch. She took a step back, apparently accustomed to and unoffended by that directive.

"And my picture collecshun." Eddie opened a small photo album with school photos of his sisters and what appeared to be his mother's wedding picture.

Eddie pointed to the handsome, smiling man in the photo. "That's my dad. He died. And he wasn't very nice."

"Do you remember him?"

"Just a little. Mostly I remember him yelling."

Sawyer touched his back in sympathy. "Your mom looks very pretty."

"She doesn't yell," Eddie said, putting his things back under his bed. "Unless she's on her last nerve. Then she yells and send us all to our room and goes into the bathtub."

Sawyer smiled at how quotable Sophie's children found her. She'd probably be gratified to know they really listened to her.

"But just 'cause somebody had a bad dad," Eddie said, sitting down beside Sawyer on the edge of the bed, "that doesn't mean he can't have another one that'll be good, does it?"

"Absolutely not."

Eddie made a face. "But nobody likes it when you try to pick out your own."

Sawyer was saved from having to respond to that by Emma, who grabbed his hand. He pretended to have to struggle against her strength.

"I have ballerinas in my room!" she exclaimed, dragging him into a pink-and-lavender bastion of femininity. There were dolls and teddy bears everywhere, and ballerinas on her bedspread and curtains.

Eddie rolled his eyes at Sawyer. "Boring, but I have to be nice to her 'cause she's my sister."

"And she did seem to appreciate your soldiers and your dinosaurs."

"Well, yeah. They're cool!"

Sawyer was introduced to each doll and bear and duly admired every one. Then a solemn-faced Gracie appeared in the doorway to tell them dinner was ready.

"This is a shortcut," Eddie said, taking him by the

hand and leading him through a laundry room piled high with clothes. "The washer's broken," he explained. "Mom's called the repairman three times, but he still hasn't come."

When they emerged from a small hallway into the kitchen, Sophie groaned. "Eddie, you didn't walk him through the laundry room!" To Sawyer she said, "I'm sorry. It isn't usually that awful. I'm going to have to break down and go to the Laundromat."

"What's wrong with the washer?"

She shrugged as she carried a basket of bread to the table. "Haven't a clue. It hums and whirrs and fills with water, then nothing happens."

"Who'd you call?"

"Ah..." She consulted a note stuck to the refrigerator with a photo magnet of the three children. "Amos's Appliance Repair."

He pointed to the wall phone above a small desk at the end of the counter. "May I use the phone?"

"Of course."

He called Marty Golden, who owned an appliance retail sales and repair shop and had donated a refrigerator and a washer and dryer to the Boy's Bunker. "Marty, it's Sawyer," he said, and told him Sophie's problem. "Can you help? Some other guy's promised to come three times and hasn't shown."

He could tell Marty was smiling. "Is she pretty?"

"Very," Sawyer replied, careful not to glance at Sophie.

"In the interest of your *pathetic* sex life—I mean you've always got somebody new, when the rest of us are fighting over the same—"

"Marty, can you come or not?" Sawyer wanted to

silence him before Marty's end of the conversation became somehow audible to Sophie.

"How is 8:00 a.m.?"

"Hold on." Sawyer put his hand over the receiver. "He can be here at 8:00 a.m. What time do you go to work tomorrow?"

"I'm off tomorrow," she replied with wonderment. "But doesn't he have other—?"

"That's perfect, Marty. I'll be on hand to meet you."

"Because you won't have gone home?"

"Good night, Marty." Sawyer hung up, then came back to the table. "All set," he told Sophie. "We're meeting at eight."

"But do *you* have to be here?" Gracie asked.

Sophie gave her a scolding look as she placed a plate in front of Emma.

"In case he needs someone to run for a part." Sawyer smiled in the face of her clear disapproval. "Would I be more welcome if I brought doughnuts?"

Eddie and Emma cheered.

"Lots of pasta and a little bit of sauce?" Sophie asked from the stove, where she was dishing up. "Little bit of pasta and lots of sauce?"

"Even pasta and sauce," he said. "You know, if you're off tomorrow, I can help you put up the flyers. The kids can come along. Maybe even Kayla. She knows a lot of the shopkeepers, so she and Gracie can take one side of the street and we can do the other."

Eddie and Emma cheered again. Gracie didn't register approval, but she didn't refuse to go, either.

"What do you think, Gracie?" Sophie asked.

"I will if Kayla wants to," the girl replied.

"All right." Sophie passed him a shaker of Parmesan, smiling widely. "Sounds like a plan."

"Garlic toast, Mom!" Gracie said as the smell of something burning suddenly filled the room.

Sophie turned in distress and grabbed two hot pads off the counter as she hurried to switch off the broiler. Smoke wafted out when she opened the oven door and removed a cookie tin of garlic toast. But only the edges of the bread were burned.

She waved the smoke away with a hot pad and asked Sawyer with a wince, "Does it look too bad to eat?"

"No," he replied, pointing to the basket of bread. "But we already have bread."

"That's because the kids don't like garlic toast and I don't usually make it just for me."

"And because she always forgets it," Gracie said with a smile for her mother. It was the first nonhostile remark Sawyer had heard from the young girl.

Sophie made a face at Gracie. The little children laughed.

"I love garlic toast," Sawyer said. "Particularly slightly incinerated garlic toast."

"What's that?" Emma asked.

"Burned," Gracie replied.

Dinner with the Fosters reminded Sawyer a lot of dinner at Shepherd's Knoll when he and his brothers were children. They talked about all kinds of things. They cracked jokes and laughed, told stories on one another. Despite their father's dark legacy, the children seemed confident about their positions within the family. Even Gracie, who was clearly affected by what had happened, had a bristling determination that would never allow her to be a victim.

And Sophie was remarkable. He enjoyed watching her deal with her children, answering all questions, backing around a few when the truth might have worried or upset them, teasing them, praising them, cajoling Gracie out of her mood.

And he loved it when Sophie looked at him. There was something a little different in her eyes. He wasn't sure what it was. Trust, possibly. Suspicion had left her gaze, and she seemed more comfortable in his presence. He was a little surprised at having an impulse to push that and see how far it extended. But she'd had a tough day all in all, and three young pairs of eyes were watching his every move.

He helped clean up, played a round of Old Maid, then decided he should leave. He didn't want to; he loved it here. And he felt entangled in their lives. He accepted with surprising equanimity that as far as he was concerned, his bachelor days were numbered.

Yet, just as Sophie was beginning to trust him, he felt himself growing less and less trustworthy. It was difficult to keep his hands to himself, difficult to know how to find the next step in this relationship.

She looked surprised as he said good-night to Eddie and Emma.

"I have a couple of hours' work to do tonight," he fibbed. "But I really enjoyed your spaghetti."

She shrugged. "It's nothing special. I'm sorry I took you away from your work. Now you'll have to stay up late."

"I'm kind of a night owl, anyway."

His remark reminded him of that cup of coffee

they'd shared at the Night Owl Café, where she'd explained why she couldn't go out with him. He was happy with the progress they'd made since then, but suspected that approaching the next phase was going to take some time.

Perversely, he was impatient.

He started to walk out to his car, then remembered that she had driven him. He turned back to see her holding up her car keys.

"Gracie, you're in charge for about ten minutes, okay?" she said, locking the front door from inside. "I just have to take Sawyer back to his car in the hospital parking lot. Don't open the door."

Gracie nodded. "I know. Bye."

Sawyer wasn't sure if that was directed at him or not, but he waved at her anyhow.

In the car, tension was high. Or maybe it was just him. Sophie chatted about various things, then told him she wasn't sure if she was more grateful that he'd saved her life or he was having her washer repaired. Then she giggled. He'd never heard her giggle. She sounded young and carefree.

Downtown Losthampton was quiet, streetlights and neon signs bright in the early darkness. The hospital parking lot was almost empty when she pulled into the spot beside his car. She turned off the motor, the sudden silence seemed to ring.

"Thank you again for dinner," he said.

"What do you like for breakfast?" she asked, opening her door as he opened his.

"Don't get out," he said, not relishing the prospect of her standing beside him in the warm, fragrant shadows of the night. His libido was strained to the breaking point as it was. "And don't make anything for me. I'll bring doughnuts, like I said, and we'll hope Marty can repair the washer. Then we'll put up the flyers, and we can take the kids to lunch at Fulio's."

She watched him with a small frown. She was probably wondering why he was listing their schedule for tomorrow as though reading an agenda. Organization of any sort was unlike him, but she made him feel he had no idea what was going on or what to do next, and he was trying to create order out of his confusion.

She looked worried. "We can manage without you tomorrow if you don't really want to come," she said.

"Of course I want to come," he corrected her. "It was my idea, remember?"

"But you were just being nice."

"No," he said candidly, "I wanted to see you again."

She expelled a little sigh that seemed to be relief. He concluded that that was good. "So, you're not finding it hard to be around me?" she asked.

He had to repeat that to himself. "Hard?" he asked.

"Yes," she said. "If I were any other woman, you could kiss me now and not worry about whether I'd scream or tremble or push you away."

Her candor made him grin. "Actually, I get that a lot, anyway."

She elbowed him in the arm. He loved how she did that. "You do not. I know that women love you. So do children."

He pushed at his door, thinking he couldn't take much more of this. She was studying him with a sweet look that was still both wary of and interested in the possibility of a kiss.

"I've got to go," he said quickly. He got out of the car and walked around it to his, only to find her standing in front of his door. "Sophie..." he warned.

SOPHIE WASN'T ENTIRELY SURE what she was doing, but her mind was replaying images of Sawyer holding her in Jack's office, replaying memories of how it felt when a man's muscle was used to comfort rather than hurt.

Now as she faced Sawyer in the soft darkness she wanted to feel his touch again. And whereas just yesterday fear would have overridden that desire, today it seemed like a test of her personal independence— a bigger step forward than anything so far.

They stood mere inches apart, his cologne, his energy wafting around her, her body leaning toward his.

"I need to know," she whispered, "that I didn't imagine this afternoon."

"You mean...Davidson?" he asked in puzzlement.

"No," she replied. "You."

"Well, I'm here," he said lightly. "You couldn't have imagined me."

"I mean that you held me."

"I did." He put his hands in his pockets. "I know that not running away was big for you."

"I never wanted to."

"Good. That's progress. So—"

She had to interrupt him. "Would you kiss me?"

He stopped to stare at her a moment. "Sophie, you're pushing yourself. You're—"

"If you don't kiss me," she said, "I'll kiss you."

She hadn't meant it to sound quite so much like an ultimatum, so she added lamely, "Okay?"

He shifted his weight, glanced up at the stars, then down at her, and said a little hoarsely, "Okay." He left his hands in his pockets.

She took hold of one of his arms and drew the hand out of his pocket herself. "Sawyer," she admonished gently. "I don't want to use you. I want you to participate."

With a sudden expression of impatience, he shook off her hand and squared his stance. "Look. I'm willing to do this, Sophie. I really am. But we're approaching this from very different perspectives. And while I can get to that gentle, tender place you're looking for, to-night might not be the best time. After hours in your company, watching you move around…"

She'd heard enough, and she could tell by how he backed away, a hand raised to hold her off, that his fear was for her and not for himself.

"Stop!" she ordered quietly.

He did, but he asked warily, "Why?"

"Because I don't want to have to grab you by your shirtfront and pull you back to me. I've experienced being dragged back to someone enough times to know it can be frightening and demeaning."

He grinned suddenly. "I might like it. There's a whole level of affection we can't indulge in because you might feel threatened. But I'm less…sensitive."

She grabbed his shirtfront and pulled him toward her, feeling wildly adventurous, as though a whole new channel of normalcy had opened in her life. She wrapped her free arm around his neck and kissed him.

It began as the kind of kiss she remembered from long ago, sweet and easy, a slow exchange of tender emotions—friendship, caring, interest. But he wasn't touching her.

A trembling was slowly building inside her, but it had nothing to do with fear. It was…eagerness, excitement, anticipation. Even she couldn't quite believe it.

SAWYER FELT HER TREMBLING as she leaned into him, and tried to draw away, not wanting to deplete her reserves of sexual courage.

"Where you going?" she asked, clasping her fingers behind his neck.

"You're shaking," he pointed out, on the brink of apoplexy with the effort to remain calm in the face of her determination to explore her feelings.

"That isn't fear," she said, kissing him again, this time standing on tiptoe for better leverage. He had to put his hands on her waist to steady her or risk ending up on the pavement with her.

When the tip of her tongue touched his lips, he wondered in mild panic if the trembling that wasn't fear could possibly be…passion?

Reluctant to believe it because that would destroy the already tentative hold he had on his control, he opened his mouth and let her explore. One of her hands went into his hair, raising gooseflesh on his scalp. The other traced down his shoulder to his chest, and stopped over his heart. It was pounding.

She pulled her mouth away from his, leaning slightly back to look into his eyes. Hers shone in the darkness.

"Are you all right?" she asked with a slightly drunken smile.

"No," he admitted in a voice that didn't sound like his. "I'd probably feel better if you'd driven over me with your car."

"Maybe you'd feel better," she suggested, running a fingertip over his lips, "if you kissed me back."

"I don't think so." He should put an end to this now, before she frightened herself. She was already worrying the hell out of him.

"How can I recover from this…limbo, if you won't show me what *you* feel?"

"Because," he replied gently, catching her meddlesome hands, "it's a little strong for this point in your recovery."

She shook her head. "I think there was more of me left inside than I'd realized. Kiss me, Sawyer."

His resistance was crumbling. "You're sure?"

"I'm sure."

He'd never been one to flaunt power or enforce his opinion, but he had always known what he wanted and was willing to do what it took to achieve or acquire it. Confidence—for good or ill—was an Abbott trait.

He finally gave it full rein.

With one hand at her cheek, his thumb tipping up her chin, he tucked her into his free arm and kissed her without holding back. He explored her parted lips, drank her enthusiasm and vitality, kissed her jaw and lingered at her ear.

"Still okay?" he asked on a whisper.

"Marvelous," she replied. "You?"

"Yes. Marvelous." He kissed her again, even more

deeply, his hands gently exploring her back down to her waist. He quelled an impulse to stroke her hip and reversed direction, instead.

Then he framed her face in his hands and drew her head back so he could see her eyes. She looked happy and smiled trustingly. "I have a terrible crush on you," she said, turning her face to kiss the palm of his hand.

"Crush?" he repeated on a laugh. The word sounded young, like that giggle.

"Yes." She leaned her head against his shoulder and expelled a sigh. "It feels simple and uncomplicated. Adoration, I guess."

"God. Sophie." He tried to hold her at arm's length, to straighten her out on a few things. *Adoration?*

But she resisted and wrapped her arms around his middle. "Oh, I know, I know. I'm sure you have flaws, but for me—right now, anyway—you're the ultimate hero. You protected me from harm, you made me feel I can be whole again, you put laughter back into my life."

Something about her absolute sincerity struck to the heart of him with equal parts of awe and terror.

He'd been asleep in the next room when his little sister had been taken. He was no one's hero.

"I'm even beginning to wonder," she went on, "if the whole stunt thing *is* because you're just fearless. It takes a very brave man to care about a woman who's locked up like a safe."

"You're not locked up," he told her, lowering his head to kiss her chastely. "You're open and welcoming. I think the scars Bill left on your sexuality are healing.''

She hugged him fiercely one long moment, then took a step away. ''I have to get back to the kids.''

''Okay.'' He had to shift gears from the subject of a crush to understanding friend.

''But I'll see you tomorrow?'' she asked.

''Eight o'clock,'' he assured her.

''With doughnuts?''

''With doughnuts. Any particular favorites?''

''Eddie and Emma love anything with cream and/or chocolate, Gracie's favorite is a raspberry-cream-cheese croissant.''

''And yours?''

''Frosted cake doughnut with sprinkles.''

He laughed. Something else to add to the giggle and the crush.

''Bye,'' she said, and climbed into her car.

As she drove away, he realized that he was in love. Big-time.

Chapter Nine

Gracie's eyes widened when she appeared for breakfast, opened the pink box and found the largest raspberry-cream-cheese croissant Sophie had ever seen.

"You told him," she accused, even as she pulled out the sweet with greedy fingers.

"I did," Sophie admitted. "Want him to take it back?"

Gracie rolled her eyes and tsked. "Mom!" The single word conveyed a long-suffering tolerance for the great gap of understanding that sometimes existed between them. "Where is he, anyway?"

"In the laundry room, helping his friend."

Childish laughter came from that direction. "Ah. The dweebs are there, too."

"Otherwise they'd be here, mooching your croissant."

Gracie sat across the table from Sophie and took a sip of her coffee. She grimaced and replaced the cup. "I don't see how you can drink that stuff." She went to the refrigerator and poured a glass of milk.

"You have to need the caffeine to appreciate it."

Sophie watched her daughter come back to the table, sipping at the milk, unconsciously graceful as she straddled her chair. She'd grown another inch since the beginning of the summer, and though she was still flat-chested and straight-hipped, the day was coming when puberty would take hold. Sophie had to get Gracie to a place in her development where she could put all the bad memories away and trust in her future.

But that was so much more easily said than done.

"You like him," Gracie said, pulling off a corner of her croissant. She popped it into her mouth and chewed, then licked her thumb and forefinger. "You looked a little dreamy when you got home."

There wasn't quite the accusation in the statement that Sophie might have expected. She was afraid to hope.

"He's a very nice man," she replied casually. "And he's been very kind and helpful to me."

She couldn't explain to her daughter that she was falling in love. She wasn't even sure how to explain it to herself. She'd been so sure that part of her was dead, wouldn't even want to be resurrected. Yet, *she'd* asked *him* for that kiss. He'd never have taken it.

She felt as though her world had pivoted 180 degrees since that day in the market when her children had told Sawyer she'd kidnapped them. She could hardly even remember how her life had been then. She'd been alone, wounded, isolated in her terminal phobia.

"Kayla says he's really rich." Gracie sipped again at her milk. "If you got married, everything would change. We'd have to move and my friends would hate me 'cause they'd think I was a snob."

''Sweetie, we're just good friends,'' Sophie replied. ''We'd have a very long way to go before thinking about spending our lives together.'' She didn't even let herself consider how far her feelings had developed in such a short time. ''That takes a lot of thought and you have to know someone really well.''

''And then you can still be wrong.''

Sophie doubted Gracie intended that to be the indictment of her decision-making ability that it sounded like. In any case, she was no longer assuming the blame for the way her marriage turned out.

''Sometimes,'' she corrected her, ''someone can change on you. That can happen to anyone. Life is filled with times when you can make a good decision or a bad one, but you always have a choice. The trouble is, most times the good decision is hard to make— you have to give up something attractive, or you have to turn away from something that seems like fun but you know will get you into trouble. The bad decisions, though, are easy to make. Steal the money, take the drugs, do what feels good because what you want is all that matters.''

''That's what Daddy did, isn't it? Stole money and took drugs.''

Gracie's question shocked Sophie into putting her cup down before she spilled its contents. She'd been so careful to keep that from the children.

''Yes,'' she admitted, hoping Gracie could handle the truth. That she had brought it up was encouraging. ''Who told you?''

''I heard Grandma and Grandpa Foster talking about it when we went to Boston for the funeral. There was an investigation or something. Grandpa said that Daddy knowing he was doing bad things is what made him mean."

"I think that's true." Sophie reached across the table to touch Gracie's arm. "But as long as we understand that, we can just forget about it and be happy with things the way they are now."

Gracie's brow frowned.

"Do you think that's wrong?" Sophie asked. "Because you have the right to feel however you want to feel about it. If you're angry at Daddy, that's okay, even though he's gone."

Instead of finding comfort in that thought, Gracie seemed to grow more troubled.

Sophie opened her mouth to encourage her to share what was on her mind, when Emma ran into the room, her mouth slathered in chocolate, a half-eaten doughnut in her hand.

"It's fixed, Mommy!" she said excitedly. "Sawyer and the man fixed it!"

Sophie took her napkin to Emma's mouth. "That's wonderful. We can spend all afternoon doing laundry."

As Sawyer walked into the room, lugging a large toolbox and looking pleased with himself, Eddie skipping along beside him and Marty Golden, Gracie left the room with her croissant and her glass of milk.

Sophie hated having missed the mark in her effort to comfort her elder daughter.

"All fixed," Marty said with a tip of his Mets baseball cap.

Sophie went to the counter for her purse. "I can't thank you enough. What do I owe you?"

"I have to work it out," he replied. "I'll bill you."

He glanced at his watch. "Got another appointment. Nice to meet you, Mrs. Foster."

"Please have a doughnut." Sophie pointed to the box.

He selected a cinnamon roll, and she handed him a napkin as she walked him out the door. "Thank you again," she said. "Three children and no way to do laundry is a terrible state of affairs."

He nodded. "You're welcome. Anything for Sawyer."

Sophie returned to the kitchen, to find Sawyer sitting at the table, Eddie on one of his knees and Emma and Hermione on the other. They were sharing his maple bar.

Sophie poured him a cup of coffee. "I've never seen anyone get such quick action. You must have real clout."

"Marty likes Sawyer," Eddie said, "'cause Marty's little boy had cancer, and Sawyer made lots of money for finding medicines and stuff. What's that word?"

"*Research,*" Sawyer replied with a shake of his head at Sophie. "This kid's radar is on all the time. It might even have Doppler capabilities."

"Tell me about it. My motto is 'If you don't want it broadcast all over Losthampton, don't do it or say it in earshot of Eddie.' What was wrong with the washer?"

"Agitator was frozen. Ate its own bolt, or something."

"Do you know what the repair's going to cost?"

"Not a clue."

"It's not," Eddie said. "Sawyer tried to give him some money and he wouldn't take it."

Sawyer pressed Eddie's jaw in the vee of his thumb and forefinger. Eddie giggled uproariously.

"I thought you'd gone to the bathroom," Sawyer said, pretending to squeeze.

Eddie laughed so hard he couldn't answer.

"You can hear everything in there," Emma, his cohort, replied. "Sawyer was gonna give Marty a hundred dollars, but Marty said no."

Surprised anew, Sawyer pinched her chin in his other hand. She screeched a laugh.

Sophie frowned at Sawyer. "He said he was going to bill me."

"He lied. He didn't want you to be upset. I'll get him back somehow—don't worry about it. And don't blame me. It isn't my fault he wouldn't charge you."

"Why did *you* try to pay him?"

"Because I thought you might have not been prepared for an unexpected expense like that. If he'd taken the money, you could have paid me back later."

She'd have continued to argue, but the roughhousing was over and both children were collapsed against him, looking very content.

If only Gracie could catch what they had.

"Are we ready to distribute flyers?" she asked, glancing at the clock. It was after ten. The stores would be open.

Sawyer stood, a giggling child under each arm. "I think so," he said, placing them on their feet.

Sophie pushed them toward their rooms. "Go brush your teeth and wash your hands. I'll send Gracie to get Kayla."

"Ever spend the afternoon with four children?" Sophie asked.

"No," Sawyer answered. "Why?"

She patted his shoulder. "It'll make your other stunts seem like a game of Old Maid."

SAWYER APPROACHED the project as if it were a military operation. Each of the three pairs—Sawyer and Eddie, Sophie and Emma, and Gracie and Kayla—was assigned a section of the small downtown.

Sawyer was explaining to Gracie and Kayla about the public events bulletin board in City Hall, when he noticed that Emma was crying.

"What's the matter?" he asked Sophie.

"I want to go with you!" Emma wept.

Eddie held firmly to Sawyer's hand. "*I'm* going with Sawyer."

"You want to come with us, Emma?" Kayla asked.

"No!" Emma was adamant. "I want to go with Sawyer."

Sophie pushed her daughter toward him and smiled smugly at him. "That's what you get for winning them over," she said. "You keep an eye on these two squirming kids while I dawdle through the dress shop, the candy store and the Antiques Attic."

"Don't forget to put up flyers!" he reminded her as she headed off. "And we'll meet up at Fulio's!"

Keeping two inquisitive children out of trouble while trying to explain to shopowners what the Annual Fair for Funds was all about was tricky, he soon realized. Some remembered it from previous years, but some had questions that required answers.

He had to rebuild a book display when Eddie wanted to see if every book in a tall stack, even the bottom one, had the same book jacket. He had to put doll clothes on a Barbie that Emma had stripped naked in the time it took Sawyer to post a flyer in the toy store's window. Then he had to stop a toy fire truck the size of a real import as it came roaring down the aisle at him, Eddie pushing from behind.

He finally split the stack of flyers in two, handed half to each of the children so that their hands would be occupied while he spoke to clerks and shopkeepers. Then he cut tape and let the children post the flyers.

Their territory finally covered, they found Gracie and Kayla at Fulio's two hours later. It was a little Italian restaurant in the middle of several blocks of antique shops, clothing stores and a host of other businesses downtown that attracted tourists in the summer. Fulio's was famous for magical pasta and scrumptious desserts.

"Any sign of your mom?" he asked Gracie.

She shook her head. "She's probably in the candy store, scarfing cherry cordials. Or in the dress shop, trying on the new fall stuff. She wants a brocade jacket. She never gets to shop without us, so she's probably having a good time."

"Okay. Then let's all have something to drink until she arrives." He called for the waiter.

Sophie joined their table fifteen minutes later with a large bag from the children's shop. She'd handed each of them a brightly colored crew hat, and one for Sawyer in khaki. Everyone pulled the hats on and laughed.

"But you don't have one, Mom," Eddie said.

She reached into the bag and put a pink one on her own head. Sawyer's heart melted. The youthful hat was a worthy addition to the giggle, the crush and the doughnut with sprinkles.

They took their time over lunch, sharing their experiences in carrying out their tasks. Then they strolled downtown in their new hats, and Sawyer bought everyone T-shirts to match them. They stopped for ice cream in the middle of the afternoon.

"Committee meeting tomorrow night," Sawyer said to Sophie. "I've drafted a press release, but I'm a terrible typist. How are you on a keyboard?"

"Not bad, actually," she replied. "And if something simple is okay, we have a basic computer. No fancy graphics or anything, but I can produce a document."

"Perfect."

He had capabilities on his computer at home to reproduce the Magna Carta, but he'd much prefer to accept her invitation.

He glanced at the children, who were all standing at the rear window, watching a backhoe terrace the hillside. "Then we're agreed it's been a great day and we want a lot more like this?"

"Yes." She pushed his cup of ice cream aside and caught his hands. "And you're okay if it takes a while to...progress?"

In a way, he wasn't. He was so eager to know what it was like to make love to her that he was sure he would implode if he didn't do it soon. Yet, he understood making love with her would commit him to a lifetime with her and her children, and the closer he got to that, the more he realized he should resolve some things in his own life first.

"I have the patience of Job."

Suddenly aware of a presence beside them, he looked up to see Gracie standing near their table, her eyes focused on their joined hands. She appeared hurt and betrayed, and her gaze at him threatened murder. Then she stormed out of the shop to the car.

Sophie groaned and watched her go with a shake of her head. She patted Sawyer's hand. "I'm sorry. She'll trust you eventually."

He wasn't so sure about that, but he kissed Sophie's knuckles and told her not to worry about it. He could endure all the glares Gracie sent his way. "I'll pick up a pizza tomorrow night."

"Great. I'll make a salad."

LIFE WENT ON FOR SEVERAL weeks in a curious state of suspension. At Shepherd's Knoll, Versace was beginning to respond to Kezia, who tossed him treats of chicken and fish. He hung out on a deep windowsill with a view of the back porch and alternately sunned and stuffed himself. He let Kezia and China pet him, but did not like anyone else. Except Emma.

Campbell and China were icily polite to each other, while she seemed to be getting a grasp of the workings of the estate that pleased everyone else.

She and Campbell, though always quarreling, did their separate jobs with such thoroughness and skill that the end result was organized and efficient. The new equipment worked as well as anticipated; the road they'd created when they moved the trees sim-

plified pruning and care considerably; and with ba-
bying, the transplanted trees continued to survive.

Though China's province was supposed to be the
books and supervision of what went on inside the
house, Sawyer noticed that she didn't seem able to
stop herself from putting on gloves and helping
Campbell in the orchard when it was clear he needed
another hand.

Sawyer sympathized with her one afternoon when
she came in dusty and perspiring. "I've asked him
over and over to let the men we've hired for that work
do it," he said. "But he's just got to get in there."

She nodded with a grudging smile. "That's the
only thing about him I understand. And I don't mind
helping out, especially in the vintage part of the orchard with the two-hundred-year-old trees. He was
almost civil today. You might keep an eye on him.
He's probably going to self-destruct, or something."

Close enough, Sawyer decided about an hour later
when Campbell walked into Sawyer's office, obviously exhausted but exhilarated. Campbell was usually so moody that Sawyer was always put on guard
by his good cheer.

"I know you haven't gotten rid of China," Sawyer
said, leaning back in his leather desk chair while
Campbell sat on the arm of a small sofa. "I spoke to
her earlier. So, what are you smiling about?"

"I got a call from Flamingo Gables," he replied.
"I interviewed there last month, remember? In Florida?" At Sawyer's nod, he went on. "The guy they
hired didn't work out and they asked me to come back
and talk to them again."

"Are you on a short list," Sawyer asked, wishing Killian were here, "or are you it?"

Campbell shrugged. "Not sure, but I know the old man liked me, and I got along all right with his two daughters." He waggled his eyebrows. "Coltish brunettes dripping with glamour and style. I could be happy there."

Sawyer wondered gravely if he could be truly happy anywhere. But it was his life. He hoped Killian would come home before he had to explain to him that Campbell was gone.

"Killian and Cordie are in London," Sawyer said conversationally. "You should give him a call."

Campbell shook his head. "I'm not going to be talked out of it. And it's not as though I'll never be back."

"Okay. Just a thought."

"Dinner's ready," China announced from the doorway.

Sawyer would have gasped in shock if Campbell hadn't done it first.

She wore a red evening dress, thin straps holding up a form-fitting top that revealed a slight swell of breast. The skirt was full and short, her dainty feet in shoes that matched the dress a wonder to behold. She'd worn slacks around the estate and a dress only occasionally at dinner. She'd been an unknown quantity so long that he hadn't really noticed she was quite a woman.

After his initial shock, Campbell relaxed and asked coolly, "Is this your lady-of-the-manor dress?"

"No," she replied, a lacy white shawl hooked in

one finger over her shoulder. "This is my going-out-with-Brian dress."

"He's your brother," Campbell reminded her.

"Actually, he's not." She'd started away and turned back to focus on him. "We're related only in spirit. He's a blood relation to Sawyer and Killian, but not to you and me. Good night."

Campbell's only comment as he headed upstairs to wash for dinner was "What a brat."

OVER THE NEXT WEEK, Sawyer spent every evening with Sophie and her children, sometimes at her home, sometimes out, occasionally at Shepherd's Knoll for dinner.

Gracie seemed to like China, and usually spent the time with her in her room, trying on clothes and experimenting with makeup. Emma loved Versace, and usually sat in a big chair in the family room with the cat in her lap, watching one of the children's videos Sawyer had bought for their visits.

Eddie barely left Sawyer's side. When Sophie insisted on helping Kezia cook or clean up, they walked around the estate, Eddie interested in everything. Occasionally, he would take Sawyer's hand in a companionable way that made Sawyer feel even better than when he completed a difficult stunt and knew he'd made a fortune for charity.

Sophie and Sawyer were in love. There was no other way to put it. They hadn't "progressed," to use Sophie's word, but they'd drawn closer emotionally. Sharing children, he realized, made that happen quickly. He'd now seen her children in moments when they weren't angelic, and had helped her quell rebellion on several occasions. He was careful not to overstep the meager authority afforded him as her friend, but found that a word from him could lend her support in a confrontation.

Awareness of their father's behavior made the whole thing very tricky. Gracie was now sometimes civil to him, but she never got within touching distance, and she loomed like a slight but dark presence whenever he kissed or touched her mother.

He was wondering one night if the status would ever change or if Sophie had simply been optimistic. Sophie had invited him for dinner, and he'd received his usually warm greeting from Eddie and Emma. Gracie, though, had been in a mood for days and ignored him completely.

They all sat around the table as Sophie served sloppy Joes and salad. She was coming toward the table with a pitcher of iced tea when Eddie, without warning, decided to run to the bathroom. He shot up, tripping her. The iced tea flew out of her hands as she and Eddie struggled for balance. The child recovered, but she collapsed with a thud as most of the contents of the pitcher landed against Sawyer's chest.

He rose out of his chair, shocked by the half gallon of icy tea that had spilled on him. Then, like someone watching a film in slow motion, he saw fear register on Gracie's face as she put her hands up to cover her mouth. Horrified, her eyes wide, she ran to her mother and stood protectively over her. "Don't!" she screamed. "She didn't mean it! It was an accident!" She began to cry. "Please! She didn't mean it."

It took him a second to realize what had happened—and what experience with her father had made her believe was about to follow.

"Gracie..." Sophie said, trying to catch Gracie's arm. "It's okay...."

But Gracie wasn't listening. Some old image playing itself out in her head convinced her that her mother was in danger, and she hovered over her, intent on shielding her. "It was an accident!" she said over and over. "She didn't mean it."

Sawyer quickly responded. "Gracie, I know that. I'm not going to hurt her. I want to help her up and make sure she's okay."

She put a hand out to keep him away. He used it to take hold of her.

She screamed.

"Sawyer..." Sophie cautioned worriedly.

He ignored her, convinced that Gracie would never believe he wasn't going to hurt her until he proved it.

"Gracie." He held her arms loosely without allowing her to escape. "Am I hurting you?"

"You won't let me go!" She had screwed her eyes shut and pulled against him.

"Right. So stop struggling and listen to the question. Am I hurting you?"

It took a minute for the question to get through. She stopped struggling, then said with a sniff, "No."

"Okay." He continued to hold on. "I never will. And I'll never hurt your mother, I promise."

He let go of her and she folded her arms.

Sawyer pulled Sophie to her feet.

"Are you all right?" he asked, tracing his hands over her, testing for injury.

"Yes." She flexed her shoulders, then winced.

Sawyer turned her to see a scrape on the back of her upper arm, which must have made contact with the corner of the hutch when she went down.

"Gracie, do you have first aid cream and a bandage?" he asked.

"Sawyer, I'm a nurse..." Sophie started to remind him, but stopped when she realized Gracie wasn't listening to him.

"My father changed," Gracie said in a tight, high voice.

He took her chin in his hand and leaned down to her. "I know about that, and I'm sorry it happened to you. But I'm not him, okay? I would never hurt any of you, and that will never change. Now, go get me something to put on this scrape."

She studied him one more moment, then hurried off to the bathroom. Emma, with Hermione, ran after her.

Sawyer put Sophie on a kitchen chair and Eddie came to wrap an arm around her neck. "Are you okay, Mom?"

"I'm fine," she said, plucking at the soaked front of Sawyer's shirt. "But Sawyer's pretty wet. I'm sorry," she said, her eyes brimming with tears. "Are you okay?"

"Of course I am." He went to the sink, squirted a little liquid soap on a wet paper towel, then returned and dabbed at her arm. "Her reaction is completely understandable."

Eddie hugged Sophie a little tighter and punched Sawyer's arm in a guy-to-guy gesture. "I know you wouldn't hurt us."

Sawyer patted his head. "Good man, Eddie."

Gracie returned with a tube of antibiotic ointment and Emma handed him a bandage. He applied the ointment, then covered it.

"There," he said. "Everything else okay?"

"I think so." She kissed Eddie's cheek. "You okay, Ed?"

He nodded apologetically. "I guess I shoulda said I was getting up."

She kissed his cheek. "A little warning would have been good. Now…"

She looked at the dinner table, which seemed remarkably intact except for a few splashes of tea. The linoleum, however, was a puddle of tea and melting ice.

Then she focused on Sawyer's shirt. "Dinner's okay, I think, but you can't sit in that drenched shirt and I don't have anything that fits you."

He had to grin. "That's a mercy. Why don't I just go home, and we can have dinner another—"

"I'll bet Jack has something he could borrow," Gracie said. She wasn't smiling, but she wasn't glaring, either. "Want me to go ask?"

Sophie nodded. "That would be good, Gracie."

She took off at a run.

Sawyer mopped up the floor while Sophie put dinner back in the oven and made another pitcher of tea.

"That was my subtle way," she said under her breath after sending the children off to get paper towels to wipe off the chairs, "of helping you cool your ardor."

He winked. "It didn't work."

She wrapped an arm around his neck and kissed him quickly. "Did you know you're the dearest man in the whole world? Possibly even beyond our galaxy?''

He straightened, his hands on top of the mop handle. ''I've thought that for some time, but I can't get anyone to corroborate it. Maybe I'm not paying enough.''

The front door opened and Gracie hurried in with a neatly folded pair of jeans and dark blue sweatshirt. She gave them to Sawyer. ''Molly says the sweatshirt'll fit, but the jeans might not. Jack says you're probably fatter than you look.''

The fear was gone from Gracie's eyes, but that troubled look remained.

''I don't supposed you defended me,'' he teased, hoping to see that expression go away.

It didn't, but she smiled thinly. ''I told him he wasn't fat. That seemed like the polite thing to do.''

''Very well done,'' he praised. ''Thanks for getting them for me.'' He handed her the mop. ''Want to finish up?''

She made a face at him, but it was only playfully hostile. At least, he hoped so. He went into the bathroom, pulled off his wet clothes, tugged on Jack's sweatshirt and climbed into Jack's jeans. There was room in the waist, but the belt from his pants solved the problem. The length was right.

Sophie put his wet clothes in the washer. ''You knew this was going to happen, didn't you?'' she asked as she set the controls. ''And that's why you got Marty over so quickly.''

He laughed. ''Sorry. No psychic abilities on my part. It was just very good luck.''

They were about to finally sit down to dinner, when

the telephone rang. Gracie snatched up the cordless, read the caller ID display and handed it to her mother. "It's the hospital," she warned.

Sophie answered the phone with a worried look at Sawyer. "Hello?"

She listened for several minutes, glancing at her watch. Then she untied her cobbler apron. "Okay. I'll have to see if my neighbor can watch the kids. How many children? Oh, God. Okay. I'll be there as quickly as I can."

She handed the phone back to Gracie, while everyone stared at her, waiting for an explanation. "A bus driving kids home from summer camp collided with a truck, and the ER is swamped. No fatals, so that's good, but lots of hurt children. I have to help." She added as an aside to Sawyer, "I'm sorry. Just stay and eat, then lock up when you leave." To the children, she said, "I'll call Molly and see if it's okay for you guys to go over. You can just take your plates—"

"No," Sawyer interrupted. "I'll stay with them."

"But I don't know how long I'll be," she objected. "It could be all night."

"We'll be okay." He turned to the children. Eddie and Emma were already jumping up and down at the idea of having him for a baby-sitter. They were so good for his ego. Then he remembered Gracie, and said, "Maybe Gracie would rather—"

"I'll be fine," she replied, looking as though that wasn't entirely true. "I'll pack you a lunch, Mom," she added, and ran off to the kitchen.

Sophie hugged him quickly, then went in search of her purse.

Sawyer encouraged Eddie and Emma to sit down and eat before dinner got cold.

Gracie came out of the kitchen with a sack lunch as Sophie appeared with her purse over her shoulder and a jacket over her arm. She kissed Gracie. "Thanks for doing that for me, sweetie," she said. "You're sure you wouldn't rather go to Kayla's?"

Gracie shook her head and indicated Sawyer. "He might need help with the dweebs."

"Okay." Sophie kissed Eddie and Emma, then Sawyer walked her to the door. "Gracie knows all their routines, but if you get into trouble, the hospital is number one on the speed dial on the kitchen phone."

"We'll be fine," he insisted. "Don't fret."

She stopped on the second step down and returned to him, affection in her eyes he could have happily drowned in.

"Can I say 'I love you'?" she asked.

If her trust made him feel terror, this took it to a new level.

"Do you mean it?" he asked.

"Most definitely," she replied.

He braced himself—he was the local master of daring-do, after all. "Then by all means, say it."

She put a hand over his heart. "I love you."

God help him. He covered her hand with his. "I love you, too."

With the children at the hospital in urgent need of care, they had little time to explore what that meant to them. She gave him one last, loving look, then ran to her car, started the motor and roared off.

She loved him. What did he do now?

Chapter Ten

Gracie served up dessert and helped him clear the table, but he got the distinct impression she was guided by the conviction that he couldn't possibly do it himself, rather than by an eagerness to help.

"They're supposed to go to bed at nine," she said of her younger siblings as they batted a Nerf ball around the kitchen.

Eddie heard her. "*She* has to go to bed at ten! And she has to keep her music down."

Gracie rolled her eyes.

"I thought we'd just not worry about bedtimes tonight," he said. He had to make himself a hero if he was going to keep the little ones on his side and win Gracie over. "Since it's been such a weird evening. There must be some movie on TV we can all enjoy."

Eddie and Emma ran into the living room, cheering loudly.

Gracie studied him consideringly. "If we went to bed, you'd have peace and quiet."

"I live in a house full of people," he replied. "I wouldn't know what to do with peace and quiet. Is there any popcorn?"

"Yeah. Healthy stuff. Low-fat."

He grimaced. "Can we put butter on it?"

She studied him again, a frown deepening. "We like it better that way, but Mom says it isn't healthy. She only does it sometimes."

"Let's make it one of those times," he said.

She dug into a drawer and handed him a microwavable packet. Popcorn was one thing he knew how to prepare. He stuck the packet in the microwave, hit the popcorn button and took the stack of plastic bowls Gracie handed him.

She put a cube of butter in a bowl and melted it when the popcorn was done. They distributed it evenly into the four bowls. Then she poured pop into glasses and placed everything on a tray.

Eddie and Emma were sprawled on the floor, already glued to the Disney Channel. Sawyer placed the tray onto the coffee table and the little ones swooped. He sat in the middle of the sofa and was flanked by Eddie and Emma, who sat as close to him as possible without actually being on him.

Gracie sat in the big chair near the sofa.

They watched cartoons, music, children's drama.

Emma fell asleep, clutching Hermione, her head against Sawyer's arm, her little mouth open like a feeding fish. Eddie, a leg slung over Sawyer's knee, struggled to stay awake.

"Why don't you go to bed?" Gracie asked. "Haven't we had enough of Disney for one night?"

Eddie looked at her as though she was insane. "No. And we don't have to go to bed, 'cause Sawyer said so."

Gracie perused the television schedule. "Come on, Eddie. There's MTV, a couple of movies…"

Afraid MTV wasn't a good idea at her age, Sawyer took the remote from the coffee table and asked, "What movies?"

"Um…" She perused the list. *"Chainsaw Massacre…"*

"Yeah!" Eddie said, changing his mind.

"No," Sawyer vetoed. "What else?"

"Desire in the Dust."

"I don't think so."

"Hope Floats!" she read excitedly. She smiled at him with enthusiasm for the first time in his recollection. "Oh, please! I love that movie. Molly has the DVD."

Sawyer hadn't seen the film, but knew it was a chick flick. He was doing this for Sophie, and because he didn't want to douse Gracie's excitement. He changed the channel.

"Is it about boats?" Eddie asked as he got comfortable again beside Sawyer.

"I don't think so," he replied.

Eddie was asleep before the titles were finished. The movie turned out to be a warm story about a single mother who rebuilds her life with her young daughter after discovering that her husband has been cheating on her with her best friend. She and her daughter move into her mother's home in Texas, where she picks up the threads of an old relationship.

Sawyer was happy with the choice for Gracie's sake until the story reached the point where the father returns for the grandmother's funeral, and the child is convinced he's come to take her back. She puts her small suitcase and a few precious possessions in the trunk of his car and he pulls them out. She tries to climb into the passenger side, but he locks her out, telling her he loves her and wants to be with her, but he needs this time alone with his girlfriend.

And then he drives away.

The child cries and screams for him until her mother takes her into the house.

Gracie was sobbing. Sawyer turned the TV off, horrified that he'd done damage to Gracie's delicate psyche by letting her watch it.

"No, no!" she shouted at him. "Put it back on!"

"But it's upsetting you."

"She's going to be fine!" she said, pointing to the television. "She figures it all out. Please."

He turned on the TV again, wondering how he was going to explain this emotional reversal to Sophie. To his shock, Gracie came to push the sleeping Emma's feet aside and squeezed between Sawyer and her little sister.

She said nothing, just sat there with the pillow she'd clutched throughout the movie and continued to watch.

"Are you okay, Gracie?" he asked.

"Yeah," she replied, dabbing at her nose with a balled-up tissue.

The movie went on for another few minutes, then everything ended happily for the child, her mother and the old flame. It was now well after midnight. Gracie heaved a sigh.

Sawyer suspected she wanted to talk, but he was reluctant to appear intrusive if he was mistaken. He muted the television.

"Does your mom have cocoa?" he asked.

She nodded. "We've got the instant stuff."

"You want some?"

"Yeah."

He moved the sleeping Eddie onto a pillow at the end of the sofa, and Gracie extricated herself from Emma and followed him into the kitchen. She pulled a box of cocoa packets from the cupboard, then reached for two cups while he filled the kettle and put it on the stove.

She put the cups on the counter beside the stove while he turned on the burner.

"Do you think she was stupid?" she asked, glancing up at him with her blotchy, tearstained face.

"Who? Bernice?" Bernice was the child in the movie.

"Yes. For loving her dad, anyway, even though he cheated on her mom and wouldn't take Bernice with him?"

Oh, no. He couldn't quite see how this connected to Gracie's issues, but clearly, it did. And he imagined his reply to her question could be critical to how she viewed the rest of her life. He wished desperately that Sophie were here to give her an answer. Sophie seemed always to have a solution to every problem, and the right words in good or bad times.

But she wasn't and he was.

He turned away from the stove and leaned a hip on the edge of the counter beside Gracie. She added cocoa powder to the cups and sniffed, waiting.

"I don't think love is ever the wrong way to react to anything," he said. "As long as you understand that some people aren't dependable, or aren't safe to be around, or will take advantage of your willingness to forgive them. You can love them because you have good memories of them, or because they were a part of your life at a happy time, but you have to stay smart and be realistic. You have to know you can't trust them to be the kind of people you really wish they were, and be determined that they're not going to hurt you again—emotionally or physically.''

She nodded and her face crumpled. Deep, gulping sobs came from her without warning. He couldn't remember ever being so terrified, but some protective instinct took over.

He put an arm around her. "What is it, Gracie?"

She continued to sob and tried to say something that was completely unintelligible except for the word *dad*.

"What about your dad?" He leaned down to hear her.

Her eyes were enormous and filled with guilt. "I loved him," she forced out between sobs. "He hurt my mom. Her mouth was bleeding and she had a cut over her eye, and he was always screaming at her…" She was growing desperate with her confession, so he drew her closer, not sure if it was wise to stop her. Something she'd buried for a long time was painfully forcing its way out. "And…and when I went to help her, he pushed me, and I told him I hated him." She paused to sob. He just held on. "But I didn't really. I loved him, anyway, even after all the bad things he did. Even after Mom was bleeding. That makes me bad, doesn't it?"

"No," Sawyer said quickly, firmly. "It's never bad to love someone, even when they do bad things," he repeated. "And he was your dad. It could be that you loved what you wanted him to be rather than what he really was."

"He was really mean to Mom."

"I know."

"She said it was okay to be mad at him and I was. But I remember when I was little and he let me ride on his shoulders and when he'd catch me at the bottom of the slide."

"It's good that you have nice memories of him."

She drew a breath and swallowed. "But you know what isn't a nice memory?"

He could see in her eyes that sharing this was going to hurt her further. He wrapped both arms around her. "What?"

She wound her skinny arms around him as far as she could reach. "When I told him I hated him, he left, and Mom put us all in the car and we went to a shelter. We never saw him again." Her voice grew tight. "And then he died, when the last thing I ever said was 'I hate you!'"

She sobbed anew, and he rested his cheek on top of her head, grieving with her for all she'd suffered. But he wouldn't let her believe that her father's pain—if he had indeed suffered any—was her fault.

"You have to understand something important about that," he said. "It's wonderful that you loved him, anyway, but because of the bad way he treated your mom, you had every right to hate him. And if he thought you did, it's because he knew what he did was wrong, but he wasn't strong enough to make himself be different. That's *his* fault, Gracie, not yours."

She stopped crying finally and said in a hoarse voice, "It's still sucky."

"Yes, it is. But if you remember those good things—riding on his shoulders and going to the park—I'll bet he remembered them, too."

She sniffed and began to relax, still leaning into him. "You think so?"

"I do."

The kettle whistled and he turned off the burner and moved the kettle off it.

Gracie dropped her arms and took a step back from him. "You probably think I'm a big baby."

"Not at all," he denied. "I think you've been very brave."

She stayed beside him as he poured boiling water into the cups. "Kayla thinks she's very sophisticated," she said, "but I know more bad stuff than she does."

"And you know that knowing bad stuff doesn't make you bad?"

"Yeah."

"Good. Anything else you've been worrying about?"

He was drunk with power because that troubled look was gone from her eyes. He'd witnessed a miracle. He might even have helped make it.

"There is something," she said, handing him his cup.

"Thank you." He braced himself again. He'd hoped she'd say no. "What is it?"

"If you married Mom, would you really want three kids?"

The question was a little scary, but he'd spent the

better part of two weeks with the little ones climbing all over him and Gracie revealing to him what she'd even been reluctant to tell her mother. He gave himself a moment to consider whether he could deal with children all the time, and was surprised to realize he could. That was very scary.

"If I married your mom," he replied, "I'd want everything that went with her."

Gracie looked grim suddenly. "I haven't been very nice to you."

Aware there was no way to blame her for that, he said simply, "Really? I hadn't noticed."

She punched his arm in a gesture that reminded him of her mother. "*While You Were Sleeping* is on next," she said with a smile, her eyes clear. "Want to watch that?"

"Sure." He followed her back into the living room, already on chick-flick overload, but relieved to see her smiling.

SOPHIE LET HERSELF into the house shortly after 2:00 a.m., still pumped from the adrenaline rush of helping treat eighteen eleven- and twelve-year-olds who'd suffered only minor injuries. The smiles of relief on the faces of parents who'd rushed to the hospital, not sure what they'd find, had been a great boost to her spirits.

Now all she had to do was repair the rubble from her ill-fated dinner, and maybe get a little sleep. She wasn't tired at the moment, but Emma would be up at 6:00 a.m. and she tended to have cookies and pop for breakfast if Sophie wasn't up, too.

She was alerted to the fact that no customary night-time routine had been followed when she heard the television. She put her jacket and purse on the credenza and walked into the living room, spotting the back of a familiar blond head over the back of the sofa. She walked around the sofa and expelled a little gasp of surprise when she saw Sawyer and her children. They were all fast asleep, looking like an ad for a Father's Day portrait.

Eddie lay on his back on the nearest cushion, his legs resting in Sawyer's lap. Gracie sat up on Sawyer's other side, her head leaning against his upper arm, Emma and Hermione sprawled in her lap.

Sophie couldn't stop staring.

At last, disturbed by the sound of the television, she took the remote from the coffee table and turned off the infomercial. She saw four bowls, each with a few unpopped kernels of corn in them, four glasses, then two cups that smelled of chocolate.

She studied her seemingly contented children—amazed to find Gracie among them—and thought wryly that they didn't appear to have missed her. Clearly, Sawyer had been more up to the challenge of coping with them than she'd thought.

And she'd felt guilty that she hadn't found time to call tonight and lend moral support!

"Hi," Sawyer said quietly, opening his eyes. "How are the little campers?"

"All well. The most seriously injured fractured his leg, but it was a simple break and he'll go home tomorrow." She perched on the edge of the coffee table in front of him. "Looks like you fared well."

He smiled. "I just let them watch anything they

wanted. You may have to explain a few scenes of *Silence of the Lambs* to them.''

She wasn't sure whether to believe him or not. They did appear as though they'd been indulged to the limits of their sensibilities. ''You didn't!''

''Of course I didn't.'' He sat up gingerly, pushing Emma's head gently onto her sister's shoulder. ''We watched the Disney Channel, then *Hope Floats*. The little ones were already asleep by that time.'' He tipped Gracie slightly toward the side, raised Eddie's legs and slipped out from under them, then let them down. He stood and took a moment to stretch and flex his muscles.

''I don't know why she loves that movie.'' Sophie frowned at her older daughter. ''It's great, but it always makes her cry.''

''I know why,'' Sawyer said, giving her a teasingly superior glance, ''and if you're nice to me, I'll tell you.'' He lifted Emma carefully off Gracie. ''Want to get doors for me?''

She preceded him down the hall and opened Emma's door, then put on a bedside lamp as he placed Emma in the middle of her bed. Sophie pulled Emma's shoes off, then drew the bedspread out from under her and covered her.

Emma made a sleepy sound, rolled onto her side, effectively smothering Hermione, and didn't even open an eye.

Sophie turned off the light.

They did the same with Eddie, then returned to the sofa, to find Gracie sitting up, not quite awake.

''Mom?'' she said groggily. ''How are all the little kids?''

"Fine. Some of them went home tonight. A few of them are going home tomorrow."

"What time is it?"

"After two."

Gracie blinked heavily and smiled. "Cool. Have I ever been up at two before? Except for the night we went to the shelter?"

"I don't think so. Come on. I'll help you get to bed."

"Where's Sawyer?"

"Right here," he replied, stepping around from behind her and offering her a hand up. To Sophie's complete surprise, she accepted it. Then, to Sophie's total shock, Gracie reached her arms up to give him a hug. "Good night, Sawyer," she said with a yawn, as though she'd been saying good-night to him for years.

Sophie stared at him.

He gave her that superior look again. "I'll make a fresh pot of coffee," he said, and disappeared into the kitchen.

Gracie kicked off her shoes beside her bed and fell back against the pillows as Sophie covered her.

"Everything work out okay tonight?" Sophie asked as Gracie yawned again. "Did Eddie hog the remote?"

"We watched a lot of Disney," Gracie said without opening her eyes. "But it was okay. Then I got to pick a movie."

"Hope Floats?"

Gracie opened her eyes, but there was no adolescent-to-adult challenge in them. "He told you?"

"That you watched the movie."

Gracie faced her. "We talked about Daddy a little bit."

"You did?"

"He said I'm brave."

"You are. I've always thought that."

"If you get married, he wants everything that goes along with you."

"Really."

"Yeah." Gracie closed her eyes and settled comfortably into her pillow. "'Night."

"Good night, sweetheart." Sophie shut the light out, closed the door quietly and went in search of Sawyer.

She found him pulling cups out of the cupboard. She took the cups from him, placed them on the counter, then dragged him back to the sofa and pushed him gently onto it. "I want to know what you talked about. Don't leave out anything."

She listened in disbelief to his explanation of how Gracie had brought up her father after the movie, and asked Sawyer what he thought of the movie child's love for her father. Of how Gracie had then shared her fears about whether her loving her own father made her a bad person, considering what he'd done to Sophie. That she'd worried about him dying thinking that Gracie hated him.

Sophie's eyes filled with tears. "So *that* was what was behind that besieged look she's worn so often lately."

He nodded. "It seemed to go away after she talked about it."

Sophie pieced together what Gracie had said with Sawyer's explanation of the evening and could imagine what a relief sharing those concerns had to have been for her.

"I'm grateful you were here to listen," she told him sincerely, "but I can't imagine why she never confided in me. I'm always telling her that her feelings are okay, whatever they are."

"She knows she can talk to you," he said, taking her hand. "But she thought her feelings were disloyal to you. She didn't want you to think she was bad. She kept telling me how mean he was to you. She's very aware you've suffered, and was afraid loving her father would contribute to that. And she's worried that he died thinking she hated him."

"What did you say about that?"

"That if she had good memories of him, he had them of her. But if he was concerned about her hating him, it was because he knew he'd been wrong, and his conscience isn't her fault."

She stared at him, wondering if she'd have seen the situation that clearly. "Thank you for being so careful with her."

He shook off her praise. "She's a nice kid. Plus, I had issues with my mother leaving, and though our family never went through what your family's been through, I know what it's like to feel guilty for what your parent did, to be convinced it has to be your fault somehow."

She wrapped her arms around his neck, all her reluctance to touch completely gone. "I'm sorry you had such things happen to you."

He shrugged that off, too, wrapping his arms around her. "Very small potatoes, all in all. I'm sorry you were hurt."

She leaned back to smile into his eyes, an unusual lightness making her feel as though she floated. Hope? she wondered fancifully. She felt free of the past and very powerful.

"Do you have to go home?" she asked.

He raised an eyebrow at the question. "No, but aren't you too exhausted for company?"

"No." She put her hand to his cheek and just let herself absorb his warmth, let it give her courage. "Do you suppose," she went on very quietly, "that we could…?"

She paused, hoping he'd help her with this. But he simply raised a questioning eyebrow, probably having no idea what was on her mind.

She was dismayed to feel her cheeks grow hot. She was terrified, but she'd so wanted an outward appearance of calm. She tried a more direct tack. At least part of the way. "I wondered if you wanted to…to see if I've…well, if I've become as relaxed as I…think I have. You know?"

That eyebrow went a little higher and he grinned. "Why, Sophie Foster. Are you propositioning me?"

She groaned and made a self-deprecating face. "That's what it sounded like, didn't it? Actually, I wish I could promise either a delightful romp or a seriously mature, deeply moving sexual experience, but I can't. I guess I'm just asking if you're willing to take a chance that I'll even remember how it's done, or that if I do, I won't get hysterical."

He watched her indulgently as she spoke and smoothed her hair away from her face with a gentle hand.

"I just don't want you to be horrified," she went

on, "or embarrassed or…or concerned that you have any responsibility for how I react, because frankly, I think I'm fine, though I've found that I can react in panic at the most unexpected—"

He put a hand over her mouth to silence her. "You can neither horrify nor embarrass me, unless you go on issuing these disclaimers." He dropped his hand, then kissed her lips slowly. When he raised his head, he looked into her eyes, his own dark with new emotion. "Consider your lips sealed from now on," he said, "unless you want to issue instructions or tell me you're feeling wonderful, or that I'm wonderful. But all negative thoughts get no oxygen. Okay?"

"What if I panic?"

"Push me away."

She tried to imagine doing that and frowned at the blow that would be to his pride and his libido.

"I can take it," he said, reading her mind. "And if you *do* panic today, you might not panic tomorrow or the next day. It's not as if there'll never be another opportunity."

She couldn't quite believe him. She hugged him tightly. "You are wonderful."

"You might want to withhold your praise until you know for sure."

"I already do. It was a personal observation, not a performance critique." She took a step out of his arms. She was nervous, but it wasn't panic. Yet. "I have to lock up and check the kids one more time."

"You check the kids," he said, giving her a quick kiss, "I'll lock up."

She caught his hand before he could start for the front door. "You're sure you want to do this?"

"You're kidding, right?" he asked. "Do you have any idea how long I've anticipated this?"

He'd anticipated this? "Really?" She couldn't help the sigh in her voice.

"Really. Meet you in the bedroom."

Chapter Eleven

Sophie looked surprisingly serene when Sawyer walked out of the shower and into her bedroom with a towel wrapped around him. The image of her slender body in pretty but mismatched undies and glossy dark hair was reflected in the oval mirror atop her dresser. She stood against a background of green-and-yellow sprigged wallpaper and ivory lace curtains— a very modern woman in a charmingly old-fashioned environment.

He wanted her with a need so far unfamiliar to him. He'd had lovers with whom he'd shared good sex and uncomplicated relationships. He'd never had one who made him feel this almost adolescent eagerness, this willingness to explore all the mazelike paths of their relationship because he was in love and nothing was too difficult or too complex to spend the time.

But he had to remember to let her set the pace, to remain controlled and attentive so that none of the things she feared would happen.

He opened the curtains to the moonlight. She came to open the window several inches, and cool, fresh air wafted in to change the atmosphere in the slightly stuffy room.

A small, jagged scar on her shoulder caught his attention. He put a fingertip to the scar, guessing her ex-husband was responsible for it. He wanted to know, but he didn't want to bring up his name.

"From my last argument with Bill," she said softly, "when I fell against the corner of an end table."

Before Sawyer had known her well, he'd been angry that a man could hurt a woman the way her husband had hurt her. Now that he knew her courage and sweetness and determination, that scar inspired rage.

She must have read the anger in his eyes. She shook her head at him. "We're not giving oxygen to anything negative."

He was about to accept that for her sake, when he noticed another scar above the line of her panties. "What…?" he began, forgetting in his anger that he wasn't going to touch her until she asked him.

"That's Emma's fault," Sophie said with a small laugh. "She was a C-section." Then she touched a long scar under the left side of his collarbone. "What's that from?"

"Killian and me playing knights and dragons when we were little. I was the dragon."

She moved to a long, thin one on his upper arm. "And this?"

"Rappelling. Scraped my arm on the hardware on a sign."

"Where would you rappel," she asked, "that you'd encounter a sign? Cliffs don't usually have them."

"It was the Abbott Mills building in New York City." When she looked disbelieving, he added quickly, "The stunt was for charity."

She walked around him. Now he knew he was in for it. He had several from previous stunts. He told her about them before she could ask the question.

"I've imagined us exploring each other's bodies," he said as she came around him again, "but not looking for scars."

She put her lips to one on his shoulder. "I hate the thought of you doing something dangerous and death defying for the hospital fund-raiser. Please, Sawyer."

"Don't worry about that."

"Thank you." She wrapped her arms around him anew, and he failed to notice that her reply seemed like a non sequitur. He focused, instead, on her hands on his bare back, her lace-covered breasts against his chest, undoing the small simple hooks on her bra.

"I'm going to remove this," he told her, doing just that. He tossed the little bit of lace at a yellow chair. He held her gently to him, stroking between her shoulder blades, feeling the tips of her breasts pearling against him.

She made a small sound he didn't think was distress, but he wasn't certain. "Panic," he teased gently, "or just mild concern?"

"Neither," she replied, her voice a little husky. "Delicious sensations."

"Good. Can we get rid of the panties, too?"

"Sure. I've always wanted to. I got them three for five dollars at the discount store, and I've always hated them. I wish I could afford only matching stuff in pastels and—"

He leaned back to look worriedly into her eyes. The moonlight cast a faint glow on her cheeks, on the curved surface of her shoulders and her breasts. "That sounds like panic."

She shook her head. "Not panic," she said breathlessly. "Bad case of nerves."

"Isn't that close to the same thing?"

She shook her head again. "Significant difference. Nerves are in anticipation—panic is in dread. Very different. Please. Get rid of the panties."

He did as she asked, slipping the simple white nylon down her legs. She placed a hand on his shoulder for balance as she stepped out of them. He straightened and dropped his towel.

SOPHIE WAS A LITTLE surprised by how comfortable she felt. Even a bad case of nerves was a very long way from the anxiety she'd experienced every time Bill had touched her in the last year of their marriage.

She'd awakened every morning since then, remembering how that had felt. The memories had helped her realize how fortunate she was to be free. But now memories of Sawyer's touch were superimposing themselves upon the old images, and in little ways, she was beginning to forget.

As he brought her close for an embrace, she wanted to remind herself how different this was from Bill's approach, how little time Bill had taken to communicate feelings, to even notice her as anything but a sex partner.

She'd always been a cautious woman who considered all her options before she acted. She'd planned and calculated the outcome of whatever she did.

But since Sawyer had walked into her life, she'd been more in the moment than ever before. Even now, all her attempts to compare Sawyer and Bill so that she wouldn't panic, were completely wasted—and unnecessary.

Panic was nowhere on the horizon. As Sawyer's hands roved her back, tracing her spine, then moving over her hip, she couldn't think at all—of anything. Touch was everything. She swore she could feel the fingerprint on every one of his fingers as they traced the lines and curves of her body.

Her sensory receptors, unfamiliar with touch intended to seduce and arouse, were overloaded with its power.

"I'm going to carry you to the bed," he whispered.

She held on as he scooped her up in his arms. His grip was possessive as he braced a knee on the bed, held her suspended for a moment while his eyes said not to be afraid, that she was safe, then he put her down against the pillows.

She saw him in a band of moonlight, all formidable male, lean-hipped and well endowed, and she noticed in even deeper surprise that although he was already aroused, she felt pleased rather than threatened.

Her breathing grew a little shallow.

"Okay?" Sawyer asked as he lay down beside her.

"Excitement," she replied, absurdly happy. She wasn't a misfit anymore! She was cured! She couldn't remember the last time she'd felt sexual excitement.

He smoothed her hair back with a smile. "What's the grin for?" he asked.

"You," she replied, slipping an arm under him and

wrapping the other around him. "You *are* wonder-ful."

"I'm not," he denied modestly.

"You are," she insisted, hitching a knee up to rub it along his thigh. "I could just lie with you forever."

"Okay. I'm wonderful." Then he stroked a hand along her side and said, "You do understand that we can't stay like this forever? We have to proceed."

"Of course." She put a hand to his cheek. "I have no problem with proceeding. I just meant that if we extended forever the way I feel at this moment, I'd have everything."

"But it's going to get better."

"It doesn't have to."

"But it will. Are you with me?"

"Yes. Also forever."

Sawyer hadn't expected slow and careful lovemak-ing to be as pleasurable for him as it was for her. But his own joy in the process was heightened by her trust in him, her complete absorption in his every move, then her very vocal response when he brought her to climax with far less effort than he'd thought it would require. He put a hand over her mouth at one point so that they didn't wake the children.

Then there was her rediscovery of her own skills, her deliberate kisses and caresses, her touch—at first shy, then eager, even bold; her obvious pride when he entered her quickly and came to fulfillment in flat-teringly little time.

They made love again, confident in their ability to please each other. He felt her lose all inhibition, all fear of her own response, and give herself completely to the experience. Her pleasure magnified his exponentially.

But he didn't know what to make of it when they lay together in the middle of the bed and he felt her tears against his shoulder.

"What?" he asked, propping up on an elbow to look down into her face.

"Nothing." She cupped his cheek. Her tear-filled eyes glistened. "Just…release, I guess. I feel so…"

Still worried, he needed an adverb—quickly. "Yes?"

"Free. Renewed. Overjoyed. Finally safe." She issued the string of words. He was relieved to find nothing objectionable in any of them. "It's all kind of complex and…" She laced her fingers together to indicate, he guessed, how interwoven her thoughts were.

He lay down beside her again and held her close. "Just continue to feel all that. Your life's turned a corner."

She snuggled into him. "I can't quite believe it."

"But it's true."

"I didn't think it could happen."

"And all thanks to your criminal-minded children."

She laughed softly and flung an arm across his waist. "Who'd ever believe that story?"

"The police officers who arrested me for lying to them," he replied with pretended indignation.

She giggled. "They didn't arrest you—they just brought you in for questioning. And hopefully, now that Eddie and Emma have found *The One*, we won't be subjected to such experiences in the future."

"That's wishful thinking. Wait till Eddie hits puberty. Our troubles are just beginning."

She raised her head. "*Our* troubles? You did say 'our troubles'?" She glowed in the darkness.

"I did. Tell me you're not surprised."

She crossed her arms on his chest and leaned her chin on them. "Caring about me is one thing. Wanting to help me care for my children is something else."

"I don't just care about you—I love you," he corrected her, stroking her elbow.

"And everything that comes with me?"

"Yes."

She used her arms on him to boost herself until she could reach his lips. "It's sometimes hard for me to believe you're real."

"Want me to prove it again?" he asked.

They made love a third time, then slept for several hours, all entangled.

When he awoke at seven, the house was still silent. The children would probably sleep for hours after their glut of television last night. Sophie stirred beside him as he swung his legs over the side of the bed.

"Where you going?" she asked.

"I should go home before the kids get up." He leaned back toward her to kiss her good-morning.

"Want me to make you breakfast?" She curled sleepily into him, and he needed all his reserves of willpower to push her back to the pillow.

"No, thanks. I've got a foundation meeting this morning at eight. You go to sleep, and I'll call you later."

"Okay. I love you."
"I love you, too."

SAWYER DROVE HOME from Sophie's with a weird sense of having just grown up—finally. Until sometime last night, his life had been about living for himself and for the foundation. He'd never considered himself particularly selfish because he did give his all to see that Abbott Mills' philanthropy searched out the neediest causes and did the most good. He was vigilant about seeing that the money reached the people for whom it was intended.

Then he worked for charities on his own, particularly through the stunts that had gained press and support, helping the usual trickle of funds become a steady stream.

That could be his way of making up for Abby being stolen from the other side of his bedroom door, as everyone presumed. It didn't compute precisely, but in his mind the simple equation of doing good to make up for once not doing so well worked.

This morning, though, his thoughts were filled with Sophie and her children. Even he was surprised by how happy Eddie and Emma had been to stay with him, how Gracie had shared with him feelings she'd been reluctant to explain to her mother, then how Sophie had come alive in his arms and thrown off the specter of past abuse to love *him*.

He knew suddenly which direction his life was taking.

At least, that was what he thought until he pulled into the drive in front of Shepherd's Knoll and saw a white Jaguar.

Killian and Cordie were home.

Thank God, he thought. He'd hoped Killian would get back before his mother returned, so that he could explain China's presence and who she might be.

He should have known better than to think things would be that simple. He walked into the house and was surprised by a happy shout of welcome from his mother, who'd apparently just arrived home, as well. She wrapped him in a perfumed embrace, a small graying woman still bearing all the style and grace she'd brought to Shepherd's Knoll. She wore a pale green sweater and slacks, and had a wide smile just for him. "How are you, *cher?*"

"I'm wonderful. And it appears you are, too."

She caught his hand and took him to a brocade chaise, where Tante Bijou was ensconced like royalty. She was very short and very plump, with rouged cheeks, mascara, a four-strand pearl choker, a diamond brooch on a lacey dress and apricot-colored hair. And she had a brilliant smile that reminded him every time he saw her of women from another century who lived on their wits after society had left them few other options. She'd charmed many husbands and lovers, and looked as though she could charm another, despite her claims of infirmity.

China, who'd been sitting beside her, stood to allow him access. Something in her usually calm glance worried him. He waited for his mother to say something about China's presence in the house. But she didn't.

Either his mother had just come home this minute, or the revelation hadn't been made.

He leaned over his great-aunt and hugged her. She

reeled off a spate of excited French. He turned to his mother for a translation, and was surprised when China said, "She says it's about time you got home. And she asks if you spent the night with a woman."

"*Oui,*" he replied to Tante Bijou's obvious delight. He noted that the rest of the family crowded closer. But since he'd used up all his French, he left further translation to China. "Tell her she's very beautiful and has three beautiful children."

There was a communal gasp from behind him. His mother sat down on the end of the chaise, fanning herself with her fingertips. "What was that again?" she asked while China translated for him to Tante Bijou. "You've fallen in love?"

"Yeah." Campbell closed in with Cordie, who held a purring Versace, and Kezia, who'd been setting the table. They came to stand near them, everyone wide-eyed.

Accustomed to having no secrets from anyone, he admitted, "Okay, okay. I'm in love."

"But it's unrequited love, right?" Campbell asked, "'Cause…I mean, who would love *you?*"

Chloe glared at him. Then she gave Sawyer a beatific smile. "Tell us!"

"Please," Cordie said. "We want details." Cordie had wild red hair wound in a loose knot, a freckle-spattered face and a warmth that had reduced his usually controlled elder brother to oatmeal.

There was a weird tension in the air, he noticed. They all seemed eager for Sawyer to talk, and he got the impression it wasn't just interest in his love life, though they'd all doubted he'd ever settle down with someone. This was different. They were depending upon him for something.

And then he realized that Killian was absent.

Bad words filled his brain, but he kept them from being spoken.

"Where's your husband?" he asked Cordie, who wore that same look China had.

"Had to stay in London," she said, stroking the cat. "Problem in the office there the morning we were scheduled to leave." She patted her pregnant stomach, which looked considerably bigger to him than it had the last time he'd seen her. "But I have a doctor's appointment tomorrow. Killian promises to be home in a couple of days. So, what about your lady?"

He turned to Campbell, who seemed preoccupied with the Rouault over Tante Bijou's chaise.

They were expecting him to explain China to Chloe.

He was suddenly happy to talk about Sophie. "She's a nurse at Losthampton Hospital," he said. "She has three children, two of whom picked me out at the supermarket as the man they wanted to marry their mother."

"Were you with the produce?" Campbell asked. "I've always thought of you as a sort of squash."

Sawyer pleaded with Chloe. "Can you do something about him?"

She shook her head. "I have never been able to. Go on."

"The children told me she'd kidnapped them. I hid them in the deli and called the police. Truth is, she really was their mother and they were just testing my reactions in a crisis. I passed. They have a ten-year-old sister, and they live in a pretty little farmhouse at the end of Blueberry Road.''

''Oh!'' Chloe clasped her hands under her chin. ''I knew it would happen one day! But everything happens while I'm away. Sawyer falls in love. This lovely young woman—'' she indicated China ''—comes to work at our home and she speaks French! Finally someone to converse with, and I've been away much of the time she's been here.''

Everyone turned to him expectantly. So. They'd introduced China as someone who'd come to help Campbell on the estate.

Damn. Killian would be able to do this. He'd worn the mantle of firstborn all his life and he had the confidence and cleverness that went with it. The last time Sawyer had stood in for him, when he'd gone to that sleepover all those years ago, Abby had disappeared. He hadn't done very well.

''I've just made coffee and berry cobbler,'' Kezia said helpfully.

Sawyer nodded. ''Great. Let's all have coffee, and we can catch Mom and Cordie up on what's been going on. Campbell, would you bring that padded corner chair to the table and I'll bring *ma tante.*''

He scooped up Tante Bijou, who giggled like a girl, and deposited her in the chair Campbell turned toward him. Then he pushed it into the table. He tried to sit beside her, but Campbell took the chair and pointed him across the table to sit next to Chloe. Cordie placed Versace on the back of the sofa, then pushed China toward the chair on Chloe's other side.

All of them seated at last, they just stared at one

another a moment, that palpable tension rising again.

Sawyer poked at his cobbler, trying to decide how best to begin.

"Did something happen while I was gone?" Chloe asked, stirring sugar into her coffee. "I thought you all seemed a little strained when I arrived, and now I feel it again. Have I been voted out, or something?"

"No," China said. "It's more a matter of my being voted in or not." She looked guiltily around the table, then added lamely, "So to speak."

Chloe was clearly puzzled. Sawyer decided that whether or not he did it well, he simply had to do it.

"China is here," he said, placing his hand over his mother's, "because she was cleaning out her parents' home after her father died and she found some things in a box with her name on it that led her to believe she might be…Abby."

Chloe gasped, went white, began to speak but couldn't seem to find words. Then her cheeks went crimson.

"Would you get some brandy, please?" Sawyer asked Kezia.

Kezia hurried away. Sawyer encouraged Chloe to take a sip of her coffee. She reached for her cup to comply, but her hand was shaking. She turned to China to stare at her. Tears coursed down China's cheeks.

"I'm sorry," China said. "I know how upsetting it is to you, but if it *is* me…"

"Of course, of course," Chloe put a hand to her heart as she studied her. "I…I can't tell. It's hard to believe that a mother couldn't tell, but you were so small."

China nodded. "I know. The Grants adopted me when I was fourteen months old."

"That's when we lost Abby." Chloe's face was stark white again and Sawyer was beginning to worry.

Kezia appeared with the brandy, and though Chloe tried to resist, Sawyer insisted she drink it. The family chorused their support. China handed her the small snifter.

"Please," she said. "I'd feel so badly if I was responsible for your being ill."

Chloe accepted the glass from her. "You have to be Abby," she said. "You're just as I imagined she'd be—thoughtful, beautiful, smart."

"We aren't certain, Mom," Campbell put in.

Chloe brushed the words away impatiently. "But can't we find out simply? I mean…isn't it easy today to find out for sure?"

Sawyer replied, "You can have a mouth swab taken from you and from China at the hospital. We don't even need an appointment. They'll send it to a DNA lab. We'd have results in a couple of weeks."

Chloe turned to her. "How long have you been here?"

"Almost a month now," China replied. "I could have been tested against Campbell's DNA, but we all agreed we didn't want to do anything without you."

"You should have called me!"

"We wanted to wait until Tante Bijou was well," Sawyer replied, "so you wouldn't have to worry about anything else."

"But…this young woman could be my daughter!" China urged her to drink the brandy.

Chloe forced down another swallow as everyone looked at everyone else.

"You said you found things," Chloe said, dabbing at her eyes with a napkin, "that made you think you could be Abby."

"My sister and I presumed the contents of the boxes in the attic were the things the state gave to our parents when we were adopted."

"Do you have your box?"

"It's in my room." China hesitated. "Do you want to see it?"

"Yes. Right away. Go get it. *Vite!*"

China excused herself and hurried as she was directed.

"If we go to the hospital this afternoon," Chloe asked Sawyer, "when will we know?"

"About a couple of weeks."

She looked despondent for a moment, then she said with a sigh, "I suppose that after twenty-five years, I can wait two weeks."

Sawyer patted her hand. "We've enjoyed having her around." He glanced at Campbell, daring him to contradict that. "Campbell's teaching her to run the estate."

Chloe looked up at Campbell, her lips pursed. "How can you still be impatient to leave when we may have found your sister?"

"I'm not impatient to leave," he replied reasonably. "I'd just like to see what life is like out from under the influence of the Abbotts."

"You are an Abbott!"

"Maman…" he chided quietly. "Let's talk about that another time, okay?"

"If there's a possibility that I can have all my children together at the same time after all these years," she said, "I will *not* have you take off on some quest—"

"Mom." Sawyer caught her hand to stop her. "He's an adult and there are things he wants to do." He met Campbell's stunned expression at his defending him and let himself enjoy it for a moment. Then he added, "And I'm sure if China *does* prove to be Abby, Campbell wouldn't be thoughtless enough to leave without taking the time to appreciate the fact that we have her back. But you have to bear in mind that we don't know yet."

She swept away that reminder a second time. "Yes, yes." Then she took the snifter and downed the last drop of brandy.

Tante Bijou spoke, apparently asking a question.

Chloe gave her a long reply, then translated with a wry smile for her companions, "She wanted to know why I was sniping at everyone *comme une espèce de folle.*"

"A what?" Cordie asked.

"*Une espèce de folle.* A…a fool. I told her China might be Abby, then explained about Campbell always wanting to leave me and Sawyer defending him."

Campbell rolled his eyes at Sawyer. "I think we're about to be sent to our rooms."

The brandy began to take effect and Chloe leaned back in her chair, finally relaxing somewhat. "I will simply change my will," she said, "and bequeath you my bills rather than my fortune."

Campbell laughed. "I pay your bills, Mom. You've already done that."

Even she had to smile. *"Méchant!"* she scolded.

"What's that?" Cordie wanted to know.

"Bad boy," Campbell replied with a certain pride. "Heard that a lot when I was little."

"And when you were an adolescent," Sawyer contributed, "and a teenager, and in college…"

China returned with the square box.

Chloe patted the tabletop and stood. "Put it right here."

China placed it there and removed the lid. On top were the yellowed newspaper articles about Abigail's abduction, giving information about the family and the old nanny, who'd eventually quit her post in grief.

Chloe nodded over them, then put them aside. "I've seen enough of those," she said as she dug deeper into the box. She gasped as she withdrew the blue corduroy rompers Sawyer and Killian thought they remembered. She took them out and held them up, the Abbott Mills Baby label visible. "These were Abby's," she said in tearful disbelief. She clutched them to her and reached for China with her other arm. They wept together.

Campbell's eyes met Sawyer's across the table. Sawyer knew his brother was thinking the same thing that had occurred to him. Twenty-five years ago, the rompers might have been possible proof. Today, being certain they were was very difficult.

Chloe delved into the box, put aside some pieces of clothing she didn't seem to recognize, then surfaced with the rag doll.

"I made this doll!" she exclaimed, holding China again. She sobbed uncontrollably.

China sat her down in her chair, took both her hands and said, "We should make sure before we get too excited."

"I'm already excited!" Chloe framed China's face in her hands and studied it. "The dark hair and eyes are right," she said. "I don't remember that pointy little chin, but you were still a round-faced baby when we lost you."

China nodded. "Killian showed me a photo he has of all of us—" She stopped and corrected herself. "Of all your children, and even I don't know if it's me."

"Will you come to the hospital with me this afternoon?" Chloe asked her. "Sawyer will arrange for us to be tested."

"Yes, of course," China agreed. "But we have to keep an open mind."

Chloe made a scornful sound. "That is for people with no faith! We will believe you are Abby!"

Campbell gave Sawyer that worried look again.

Chapter Twelve

"Well," Cordie said, picking up her fork, "I'm going to finish this wonderful cobbler, and then I have presents for all of you from Florence."

The tension and excitement were high. They hung in the air, tightening everyone's smile, raising the volume on everyone's laughter as they tried to talk normally about Florence, Paris and all that had happened in Losthampton while Chloe and Cordie had been away.

Sawyer eventually escaped the table while Cordie distributed Italian silk scarves among the women, including Kezia and China.

China stared at hers openmouthed. "But...you don't know me. I was here only a few days when you and Killian left."

"You're important around here," Cordie said, putting a fat stack of photo envelopes on the table. "You could be my sister-in-law."

Sawyer hurried toward the kitchen while China thanked Cordie profusely. He stopped in the middle of the room, trying to decide what to do with himself, when Campbell collided with his back. He'd followed him out, looking as desperate to escape as he felt.

"For God's sake keep going," Campbell urged, pushing him toward the door. "Let's get out before they make us go back!"

They escaped as they had when they were children avoiding chores or discipline.

Sawyer led the way to the boathouse, where he kept Samuel Adams beer and other treasures in the small refrigerator.

"If this goes bad on us," Campbell said, sitting in a decrepit but comfortable old red chair they'd retrieved from the Dumpster when Chloe had remodeled, "I'm out of here. If China *isn't* Abby, I don't want to be around."

"Coward," Sawyer accused from a wicker love seat.

"Damn right. Who's going to tell Mom about Brian?"

"That can wait. Maybe Killian will be home by then."

"I wonder if he really had to stay in London, or if he just wanted to avoid all this. He had to know Mom was about to come home."

"I'd suspect that of *me,* but not of him."

Campbell raised his beer glass to him. "Actually, you were very good about telling Mom. You got right to it. I was impressed."

"Well, I had little choice, did I?" Sawyer said. "You all just hung me out to dry."

"That's the lot of the eldest. The rest of us hide behind him."

"But I'm *not* the eldest."

"While Killian's in London, saving the corporation, you're next in the chain of command."

"Yeah, well, I wish you'd all give me something fun to take charge of. Like skydiving trips or motorcycle tours."

"Motorcycle tours," Campbell repeated in surprise. "You don't even ride a motorcycle."

"I can. You just haven't seen me on one. I'm not bad."

The whole exchange had sounded innocuous enough to Sawyer, so he was surprised when Campbell focused on him with sudden interest and asked with a slow nod, "Is *that* your stunt for the hospital event?" Campbell must have guessed by Sawyer's stunned expression that he was right. "It is! How are you doing it? You're not going to jump over barrels. You already did that on skis—and finally got it right. Let's see, a wild somersault off a high ramp?" he speculated. "Through a ring of fire like a circus lion?"

Months of keeping the stunt secret, then ten days away from the arrival of the equipment and twelve days from the event, and Campbell had guessed the truth.

"Yes," Sawyer had to agree. "Through a ring of fire. Just be quiet about it, okay? Half the tickets are sold in anticipation of what I'm going to do, and the other half are sold after the news release comes out and people want to see me crash."

Campbell's brow furrowed. "Nobody wants to see

you crash. I can't explain it, but everybody likes you. They want to see you make it.''

Sawyer was skeptical.

''Oh, get over yourself. You like the danger of tee-tering on the edge of life and death, thinking you're risking everything in the name of charity, when you're just trying to prove to yourself that the man you are bears no resemblance to the scared little kid who's sister was kidnapped.''

Sawyer gave him a dark look. ''And how would you know what's in my head?''

''I was there when Abby was taken, remember? I suffer from the same thing. Only, I…keep people at a distance so no one can read it in me. You try to help people—let them get close. I'm not that brave.''

Sawyer had a heavy sense of everything familiar in his life taking a radical turn. The sister who'd been lost for so long might have been found; he'd discovered a brother; and he'd given his heart to a woman and three children, putting paid to his freewheeling bachelor lifestyle.

That all made riding a motorcycle through a ring of fire seem like picking daisies.

''Do you think China is Abby?'' Campbell asked, suddenly introspective.

''I don't know,'' Sawyer replied honestly. ''Sometimes I think so. She reminds me a lot of you.''

''Watch it.'' Campbell grinned as he said the words. ''I've never been that argumentative.''

Sawyer couldn't help the shout of laughter. ''Cam, you disagree on your own last name. You don't want to be an Abbott, but you are. How argumentative is that?''

Campbell's grin broadened. ''Okay, maybe I am a little. Did I tell you that Flamingo Gables hired me?''

''No, you neglected to mention that.'' Sawyer tried to absorb that fact with equanimity. He couldn't change it, couldn't make Cam stay. ''What if China *is* Abby?''

''I'll be home for all major holidays,'' he said. ''I've already gotten to know her better than anyone else here since I've worked with her day in and day out. But…'' That last word sounded constricted, as if he were holding in check powerful feelings. Campbell wasn't good with vulnerability. ''I guess I hope she is for Mom's sake.''

Sawyer could relate to that wish. ''It would be nice to know she is safe and sound after whatever happened.''

''Yes, it would be.''

''When do you leave?''

''They could use me right now, but I'll hold off for a week or so. I'd hate to walk away on Mom right after she got home.'' He grinned again. ''I would like to avoid Killian, though, if at all possible.''

Sawyer laughed. ''You can never avoid Killian. He'll come and find you.''

''You understand why I'm doing this, right?''

Sawyer looked into his brother's face and thought that he would never completely understand him, not in the same way he understood Killian. But then, there was a lot he and Killian had in common as older siblings that he didn't share with Campbell. But he could give him a break.

"Not entirely, but I don't have to. I can support your need to do what you have to do, whether or not I understand it."

Campbell nodded, apparently satisfied with that. He stood. "Well. I've got work to do in the orchard. Weren't we supposed to have dinner with Brian tonight?"

"Yeah. Maybe we should just invite him here and explain him to Mom. I'll call him and see what he says. I'll let you know."

Sawyer took his mother and China to the hospital shortly after lunch. While they were filling out forms prior to the DNA test, he stuck his head into the emergency room. It was empty, except for a young boy with a black eye, who was being treated by Dr. Brown. Sophie, assisting him, saw Sawyer in the doorway and waved. Her face lit up with such pleasure that he felt both humbled and powerful.

He pointed behind him to indicate that he'd be in the waiting room. His mother and China had already disappeared into an office, so he sat down with a three-month-old copy of *Boat Builder Magazine*.

Sophie appeared a few minutes later. She glanced around to make sure no one was around and kissed him quickly, her eyes and her smile bright. "I've missed you something awful!" she said, "and it's only been about eight hours."

He drew her back into his arms when she would have moved away discreetly. "Oh, I know," he teased. "The Sawyer charm is like a drug."

''I can get some pretty fancy stuff right here if that was all I wanted.''

''But can it make love to you all night long?'' he whispered.

She put a hand over his mouth and looked around again. She pretended indignation, but he could see the memories in her eyes. ''What are you doing here, anyway?''

He explained about his mother's return and the long-awaited test. ''Did you get any sleep today?''

''A few more hours after you left. Molly called to tell me the kids have talked about you all morning long. Seems you made quite an impression and are now the baby-sitter of choice. The One. Even Gracie thinks so.''

He liked that. ''Do you want to marry me?'' he asked.

She hesitated. That alarmed him for a moment, until she blinked and asked, puzzled, ''Was that a proposal, or were you just asking my opinion on whether or not I think it's a good idea?''

''It was a proposal,'' he replied, ''as long as your opinion is positive. You were so adamant when I first met you about not wanting to get married again. And I could understand that. But living together isn't a great option with three kids around, one of them a preadolescent girl.''

She looped her arms around his neck, apparently forgetting her concern about being observed. ''I would want to marry you whatever situation or condition prevailed. Yes, to my opinion being positive. Yes, to your proposal!''

She kissed him soundly. He kissed her back.

When they finally drew apart, his mother and China stood beside them.

"This must be the beautiful woman you told me about," Chloe said, moving in to give her an embrace. "I understand you're going to make my son a family man."

Sophie looked from Chloe to Sawyer in surprise. "Did he tell you that? He's only just proposed to me."

Chloe patted Sophie's hand. "He's a man of great determination. He must have been confident he'd convince you. My aunt is visiting, and China and I were thinking it would be a great evening for a party. Will you join us with your children?"

It occurred to Sawyer that they might have to save the Brian revelation for another time. Or maybe not, depending on how the evening went. He wondered idly, while the women talked, if Killian was watching all this from somewhere and deciding to stay away until all the hurdles were cleared.

Sophie walked them out to the car.

"Campbell and I were supposed to have dinner with Brian Girard tonight, Mom," he said as China climbed into the back. "If you're throwing a party, why don't we invite him to join us, instead?"

She blinked at him. "Corbin Girard's boy?"

He nodded. "Corbin recently disowned him and he's been spending a lot of time with us since…my accident." He'd slowed his explanation when he realized no one had told her about his accident.

''Ah,'' she said. ''The barrels-and-the-skis accident?''

Now he blinked. ''Yes. Who told you about that?''

''Cordie, while she was helping me unpack. I also heard about the in-line skating accident. Don't tell me you really rode one of those concrete curls and expected to turn a somersault like a twelve-year-old.''

''Yes, I did,'' he said intrepidly. ''But the event's been postponed, so I have lots of time to perfect my style. Or decide on doing something else entirely.''

''So, what's next?'' she asked. ''Annapurna without a Sherpa or oxygen?''

''About Brian…'' He wanted to distract her.

''Yes, do invite Brian. The family's always considered his father and him enemies, but I always thought he seemed a lot like the three of you—forced to adapt to a life he might not have chosen.''

Maybe explaining their relationship to Brian wouldn't be as difficult as he'd imagined. But how nice it would have been if Cordie had taken care of that, too, while she was listing Sawyer's accidents.

He helped his mother into the back of the limo, then turned to give Sophie a quick kiss.

''Seven o'clock, dear,'' Chloe called out. ''I'll send the chauffeur for you. All right, Daniel?''

''My pleasure, ma'am,'' he replied.

''All right, Mrs. Abbott.'' Sophie held the door as Sawyer climbed in beside his mother. ''Thank you.''

SAWYER SPENT THE REST of the afternoon catching up on mail, assessing requests for foundation funds and putting them aside for the board meeting. Then he took an hour off to see Lou Bergman, the mechanic who was lending him the motorcycle, and to ride the bike. It had been a few days since he'd been on it, but the feeling of control remained.

He imagined it was the same sense of power the old cowboys felt on a horse—a certain oneness between vehicle and driver that made seemingly impossible maneuvers easy.

He circled several times until the thrum of the bike's motor made his blood run to the same rhythm. Then he took the jump. He roared off it into space, imagining the ring of fire and sailing right through it. The wind grabbed him, held him aloft like a seagull on a current of air, then freed him to hit the landing ramp and finally come to a stop.

He sat there for a moment, exhilarated. The stunt was going to work. He wouldn't be able to practice the actual ring of fire until two days before the event, but it felt so right.

He washed the bike and put it away.

He showered and dressed and hurried down for his mother's big family dinner. Talk about a ring of fire!

"Wow!" Emma exclaimed. "A television!"

"And booze stuff!" Eddie said.

Sophie pulled both her children back onto the limo's rear seat and pushed the cabinet that held both TV and wine decanters closed. "I know this is all very interesting," she said, unaccountably nervous, "but because it's all so special, we have to behave in a special way. No touching everything, no shouting too loud and no acting like you're playing on the ball field, okay? We have to behave like ladies and gentlemen. We're going to meet some very special people.''

Eddie settled down beside her, his feet sticking out and hitting Gracie's knees on the opposite seat. She brushed them aside. ''Isn't it just Sawyer's mom?'' Eddie asked. ''She'll be nice, won't she?''

''She is nice,'' Sophie assured him, ''but she's also very elegant, so let's just try not to act like ruffians.''

''What's a ruffian?''

''You,'' Gracie replied. She turned her attention to Sophie with a new clearness in her eyes that Sophie was so happy to see. Gracie's sharing that fear with Sawyer had changed something in her, something that had blocked her blossoming. She seemed to be on her way now. ''Mellow out, Mom,'' she said. ''Sawyer told us he and his brother were devilish when they were little kids. I'm sure his mom's used to ruffians.''

That was no comfort to Sophie. And there were so many faces! Fortunately, her children were sociable and smiled, instead of hiding behind her the way many children would have.

Some of the family she knew. China introduced her to Cordie. ''She's expecting twins,'' she said, ''and is insufferably joyful and perky.''

Cordie took her from China so that she could meet Cordie's husband, Killian, a tall man with Sawyer's coloring but a calmer, more laid-back nature. He'd apparently just gotten home from London an hour earlier.

He was speaking with Brian Girard, who, Sophie knew from Sawyer, was their half brother.

China ushered Emma and Eddie inside to the low table where hors d'oeuvres had been set up.

Chloe looped an arm in Sophie's and led her to an Adirondack chaise on which a very old woman was seated, an embroidered shawl placed over her legs. Despite her obvious age, she looked bright and cheerful.

"This is Tante Bijou," Chloe said. "She speaks only French. I was with her for a month and a half while she was ill, and brought her home with me to help her recover. She loves to see the boys." She performed the introduction again in French.

The woman offered wrinkled, bejeweled hands to Sophie, then spoke in rapid, excited French.

"She's very pleased to meet you," Chloe translated. "She thinks Sawyer is special and says you look as though you are, too."

"Elle est merveilleuse," Sawyer said, wrapping his arms around Sophie from behind.

Sophie turned to smile at him. "I didn't know you spoke French."

"College French," he explained. "Very marginal, but when Mom's swearing at me, I like to know what she's saying."

"Oh!" Chloe swatted his arm and laughed.

Sophie was awed by the formal dining room. The large Hepplewhite table would easily seat the twelve people gathered, and could accommodate several more. And there were no odd chairs, no furniture dragged in from another room to fill in. Twelve high-backed Hepplewhite chairs stood around the table and several more sat tucked away on either side of a matching buffet.

The room was decorated in burgundy and gold, and the French doors that opened out onto a porch at the back of the house were left open. Salt air, fragrant with wildflowers and fruit from the orchards, wafted into the room.

"Wow, Mom," Gracie whispered. She sat on one side of Sophie, with Emma and Eddie on the other side of her, and Sawyer between the two younger children. Killian, Cordie, Brian, Chloe and Tante Bijou sat opposite them, with Campbell and China at either end of the table.

Daniel helped Kezia serve a dinner of capons, sweet potato straws and asparagus.

Chloe held forth, encouraging Killian and Cordie to talk about Florence and London, then asking Eddie and Emma about their summer adventures.

"Sawyer took us to put up posters downtown!" Eddie said excitedly, the way some other child might report on a trip to Disneyland.

"Big spender," Campbell teased his brother. "Did he make you do all the work?" Campbell asked with a smile for Eddie.

Eddie shook his head. "But he made me hold the posters so I wouldn't touch anything 'cause I dumped a stack of books at the bookstore."

Laughter greeted that admission.

"And Emma ripped all the clothes off a Barbie!" he added, loving all the attention. "Sawyer had to put them back on."

His brothers seemed to enjoy that story, too.

"We picked him out," Eddie added.

"Who?" Brian asked.

"Sawyer." Eddie pointed to him. "To be our dad. And he's gonna."

There was a communal "Aww!" then a round of applause.

"Gracie likes him, too," Eddie went on. "She didn't at first, but now she does."

Gracie blushed. Sophie was grateful when Eddie said no more.

Daniel poured a dessert wine while Kezia served a very elegant strawberry shortcake, using shortbread cookies in the shape of seashells and sprinkles on the whipped cream. Eddie and Emma were enthralled.

Killian stood to offer a toast. "To Mom's return," he said. "To having the pleasure of Tante Bijou's company, to the wedding in our future, to having found our brother and to China's presence in our midst. We'd like her to be our sister, but whether she is or not, she's still a welcome part of this family."

There were "Here, heres," then Chloe asked quietly, "What brother?"

"What?" Killian asked.

"You said 'to having found our brother.'" Chloe looked puzzled. "Do I have a son I don't know about?"

Killian turned from Campbell to Sawyer, but was too noble to blame them for not having told her. He simply gave them a glower that promised retribution, then explained to Chloe what they'd discovered when Sawyer was taken to the hospital.

She put a hand to her heart. "My goodness! And that was kept from us all this time?"

Brian, clearly disliking the spotlight but refusing to hide, nodded. "I only found out myself about a year ago. And I didn't think you'd want to know the truth." He quickly explained what had happened with his own mother. "But there's a rare generosity in this family, and I'm now very happy to be a part of it. I hope that's all right with you."

Chloe walked around the table to wrap him in her arms.

"Well, it's more than all right," she said, kissing his cheek. "I'm only sorry someone didn't mention it sooner so that I could have been more welcoming."

She glared at Sawyer as she resumed her chair. "Well," she said, sitting down. "Isn't it wonderful how families just blossom. Our numbers are growing. We began diminished by one, and now, here we are, almost a crowd."

The party moved outside and teams were chosen for badminton.

Sophie watched the glowing faces of her children and couldn't remember a moment when she'd felt so happy and so safe. Even remembering how dark her life had been was hard, when now all that surrounded her was love, kindness and hope.

Sawyer, with Emma on his shoulders swinging a badminton racket and Hermione safely left with Sophie, blew her a kiss. Her heart brimmed with gratitude. Sawyer's love and patience, and the delicious night they'd spent together, had erased all the thorny memories that had once entangled and confined her.

China and Cordie came to sit beside her in the grass as she watched the badminton game, which seemed to be played without adherence to any rules whatsoever. Campbell was helping Eddie, and Brian, on the sidelines, lent a hand to whomever he thought needed his assistance.

Winfield stood apart and shook his head, like a referee in a hopeless competition.

Killian and Chloe sat on the sidelines, chatting when not being entertained by the game.

Cordie shook her head as Campbell and Brian collided over a shot. "Hard to believe they're all respected in the business community and among the social elite, isn't it?" she asked.

China made a face. "I worry about that. My adopted family was wonderful, but very blue collar. If I *am* Abby, I'm not sure I'll fit in."

"You already do," Cordie insisted. "There are no snobs in this family and we don't keep company with any."

That was good news to Sophie. She was having the same fears China was. Only, there was no doubt she would have to adapt. She wasn't giving Sawyer up for anything.

Sophie ran out to the limo sometime later to retrieve Emma's sweater as the evening breeze picked up, and saw a white van pull up to the house. *Losthampton Leader*, was emblazoned on the side. A man leaped out of the vehicle, carrying a large, flat package wrapped in blue paper.

"Party going on?" he asked Sophie.

"Yes," she replied, recognizing him as the newspaper's publisher. He'd been to the hospital working on stories about budget and staffing. "Can I help you? Do you need a member of the family?"

He shook his head. "No need to disturb anyone if you'll just give these to Sawyer for me. I promised to have them to him today, but I didn't expect to be this late. Had a little trouble with one of the presses."

"Of course." She took the package from him and headed for the house with it, but on the porch she stopped suddenly, her heart stalling in her chest when she realized what she held. A sheet of the print job the package contained was taped to the top.

It was newly printed, circus-size posters to advertise Sawyer's stunt at the hospital benefit. In glorious color on glossy, large-format paper was a man in fire gear and a helmet on a motorcycle jumping through a fire ring. The sight made her blood run cold and her cheeks fill with angry heat.

"Here you are," she heard Sawyer say. She also heard the screen door slam and footsteps coming toward her, but she couldn't tear her eyes away from the portent-of-doom image on the poster. "What are you—"

Sawyer halted abruptly as she raised her eyes to him. His eyebrows went up in confusion at her expression until he looked down to see what she had in her hands.

"These were just delivered," she said flatly, struggling to get control of her temper. "He said to tell you he was sorry he's late, but they'd had trouble with one of the presses."

"Okay." He took the package from her and put the

posters on a wicker table nearby. "So, what's the problem?"

"What's the problem?" she demanded. "How can you even ask me that? Have you completely lost your memory?"

He folded his arms, clearly not getting the point. She couldn't believe him! "My memory?" He reflected none of the guilt or sheepishness she would have expected, considering he'd lied to her.

"Your memory! I said that I hated the thought of you doing death-defying stunts, and you said, 'Don't worry about it.'" She mimicked his deep voice. "I thought that meant you weren't going to do it."

He seemed suddenly to understand what she was talking about. "No," he said calmly, "it meant, 'Don't worry about it.' I'm always careful." He reached a hand out for her. "Come on, Sophie. You knew I do this all—"

She backed out of his reach. "Yes, I knew you did this all the time," she replied, struggling to remain calm when emotions were rioting inside her. "But I thought having a woman and children who love you would change your mind about these ridiculous risks."

"And it has," he said, surprising her, giving her hope. "I'll scale down. I'll do less-dramatic things. But I have to do this one."

Her hope dashed, she demanded, "Scale down? You mean you'll rappel down a twenty-story building rather than a thirty-story one? And why do you have to do this stunt?"

He shifted his weight, obviously not seeing a reason for the question. "Because the press release is in tonight's paper. It's advertised. I have to do it."

"You *have* to do it because you *want* to do it," she countered. "I don't understand what drives you about that. I've spent so much of the past few years afraid and worried about my children's safety and my own that I am not going to subject myself to watching you ride a motorcycle through fire. I won't!"

SAWYER HAD NEVER DEALT well with ultimatums, and he felt one coming. And as much as he loved this woman, he was thrown off balance by the intensity of her anger, when she was the one who'd misinterpreted their conversation about this in the first place. He also couldn't believe that after all she'd been through, *this* was upsetting her.

"Sophie, you're being unreasonable," he said quietly. "I *have* to do this. I promised. Surely you can see the importance of a promise."

She glowered at him. "You promised *me* I didn't have to worry."

"You don't. I know what I'm doing."

"You almost drowned with the waterskiing trick! You fell while in-line—"

He caught her arms and gave her a small shake. "There are risks. That's why these stunts make money for the charities. I *have* to do this. That's it."

She struggled urgently against him, a flare of fear in her eyes.

He released her quickly, holding both hands out to show he had no intention of hurting her. Lost in his own emotional response to her anger, he hadn't considered that taking hold of her would frighten her.

"I'm sorry," he said, keeping his distance. "You know I wouldn't hurt you."

She folded her arms and stood beside the porch column, looking just as rigid. "Yes, I do," she admitted in a small voice. "It was just…old instinct." She tossed her head, apparently willing to put that aside. "So, it doesn't matter to you that two little children picked you out, decided you were The One? That Gracie smiles now?"

"Of course it matters," he said impatiently. "But what also matters is that you're making this a deal-breaking issue. That's not fighting fairly."

She rolled her eyes. "Well, pardon me for not wanting to see you ignite or fall on your head, or any of the scores of other things that could happen to a man on a fuel-filled motorcycle flying through fire!" Her voice rose in proportion to her anxiety, until she was shouting the last few words.

"I told you that wouldn't happen. I've been practicing for months."

"Practice doesn't prevent accidents."

"Life involves risk, Sophie." He took a few steps closer to her, encouraged when she didn't back away. "You think because you suffered terrible things and finally got free of Bill that you never have to deal with risk again, but that's not true."

This time she grabbed him, small fists closing over the front of his shirt. "I understand life risks, but this is something you're choosing to do when you don't have to."

"I do have to," he insisted. "I promised."

"Because you need to risk everything!" She was starting to cry. He'd have happily capitulated under any other circumstances but this one. He'd promised. The press release was out. "Don't you realize you're risking *me?*"

"Do you realize you're threatening to walk away from me, when all I've done is try to give you what you need?"

"What I need is *you!*"

"You've *got* me!"

"I mean I need you safe! Not scaring me to death!"

That was all delivered at high volume, and he noticed absently that there was a collection of worried faces on the other side of the screen door, that Gracie, Eddie, Emma and Campbell stood at the bottom of the porch, silent but frowning. This discussion was too important, however, to allow himself to lose focus.

"I love you," he said firmly. "I want to marry you and be a father to your children. But you can't lock me up because what we have together is finally what you've always wanted. It won't keep me safe. I could get hit by a car tomorrow. Life is a risk."

She dropped her hands from him in disgust and swiped them over her eyes. "You're almost right. I'm beginning to see that *you're* the risk, and I'm just not strong enough to take it. Goodbye, Sawyer. Please thank your mother for inviting us and tell her we had a…a lovely time." She turned and ran down the stairs to the limo, urging the children to follow her.

Daniel opened the screen door and trailed behind her with a sympathetic glance in Sawyer's direction.

The children looked hurt, stunned, unsure what to do.

His heart twisted in his chest, Sawyer went down the steps, lifted Emma onto his hip, took Eddie's hand and smiled empathetically at Gracie. "I'm going to need your help here, Gracie."

"Okay," she said thinly, and kept pace with him as he went to the limo. Daniel had seen Sophie into the back, where she waited for her children, staring out the far window at the lawn, her sobs audible outside.

"What happened?" Eddie asked. "You're The One. Why are you fighting?"

Sawyer hugged Emma tightly, then put her on her feet and knelt on one knee in front of her and Eddie. "Even when people love each other they disagree on things."

"I know," he said grimly. "I remember."

Sawyer thought grimly that such little children shouldn't have indelibly bad memories that would come alive in difficult moments. "Not that kind of argument," he said. "Nobody's ever going to hurt her again. But sometimes even though two people love each other, they have different opinions on important things and that can't be changed. And if that happens, they decide it's better not to live together."

"But you're The One!" Eddie repeated in a strained voice.

Sawyer pulled him close. "You're the three for me,

too. We'll try to work out a way that we can still do things together.''

''No,'' Eddie objected, understanding even in his child's mind that that wouldn't work. ''We were gonna get married!''

''I know. But we don't always get what we want. That's just the way it is.'' Before the boy could offer further resistance, Sawyer put him in the car, then lifted Emma in beside him.

When he turned to Gracie, he saw tears streaming down her face. She wrapped her arms around him. ''I'm going to work on her,'' she wept quietly. ''Don't give up.''

''I'd like to fix this,'' he replied, ''but I'm not sure it can be done.''

''I hated myself and thought my life would always be horrible,'' she said, drawing back to look up at him, ''but you made me understand that that stuff wasn't my fault. Dweebie Eddie's right this time. You're The One. We're going to get you back.''

She hugged him tightly one more time, then climbed in to sit opposite her mother. Sawyer blew the kids a kiss, then closed the door.

Daniel drove away.

Sawyer's heart sank. He realized suddenly that this was what it felt like to risk everything…and lose.

Chapter Thirteen

Sophie had no idea how she got from day to day. She couldn't eat and hardly slept, and her children were heartbreakingly helpful and cooperative. They did their chores, washed dishes without complaint, and she couldn't help the feeling that lack of spirit, rather than a willingness to be model children, guided them. They didn't even seem to have the will to argue with one another.

She sat them down to explain what was wrong between her and Sawyer. She told them without going into grizzly detail about his motorcycle stunt, how she'd just gotten over being afraid and she didn't want to be afraid again.

Eddie didn't get it. "But he never hit you."

"You don't have to hit people to hurt them," Gracie said, surprising Sophie into staring at her.

"Thank you, Gracie," Sophie said. "That's exactly what I meant."

Gracie nodded, then looked away. "It's just that…I mean…we all really like him, and it's so much better when he's around than it was with Dad. He never yells or shoves. With Dad you were scared all the time. So, if you're just scared for the time Sawyer does a stunt, isn't that a lot better?''

''I'd be scared all the time, though. I love him, too, but I'd be afraid we'd lose him. I'd always be worried about the next stunt and the one after that.''

''Except we've lost him, anyway, right? Why is it different this way? Because you don't have to be afraid?''

That question jarred Sophie. When she didn't know how to answer it, she dismissed it.

She tried to make up to the children for depriving them of Sawyer by cooking and baking their favorite dishes. She enrolled Eddie in a karate class, Emma in ballet, bought Gracie and Kayla new swimsuits and signed them up for swimming lessons at the pool, then wore herself to a frazzle dropping them all off and picking them up on lunch hours, coffee breaks, before and after work.

The local television touted the hospital event and Sawyer Abbott's latest stunt, as did the *Losthampton Leader* and the radio station. Sophie couldn't turn around without encountering the facts.

She missed Sawyer with a burning emptiness in her heart and a diminished satisfaction in everything she did. She couldn't find anything to laugh about, and though the children seemed to enjoy the new experiences she'd provided for them, neither could they.

THE ABBOTT MILLS FOUNDATION gave away more money in the next twelve days than it had since its creation. The funds Sawyer had invested for the foundation in real estate investment trusts had survived even the e-market collapse, and done so well that he was able to supervise the deployment of small fortunes to worthy causes all over the country.

The foundation set the funds to build a teen shelter in a small town in Oregon; gave money to a small theater group in Wisconsin that ran summer camp for disadvantaged youth; helped rebuild a church in Georgia that had been destroyed by fire and made a substantial contribution to a program that granted wishes for dying children.

Killian walked into Sawyer's office at home the afternoon before the hospital event. Sawyer had been riding the bike all morning and was tired and bad-tempered. All the work he'd put into the distribution of funds had done nothing to fill the giant hole in his being the loss of Sophie and her children had caused.

"I was working on collecting data for the monthly report," Killian said, "and wondered if this figure was correct. The foundation's given away three million dollars in the past two weeks?"

"Right," Sawyer replied. "We made money on some real estate investment trusts, and I suddenly thought, why sit on it? Let's get it out there where it can do the most good."

Killian nodded his agreement. "Good thinking, but what happened to your careful analysis of every detail of distributing money?"

"I did quick checks," he said. "I just decided that maybe I should be more trusting."

"Ah." Killian sat on the window seat. Oh, no. He wanted to talk. Sawyer always hated that. It forced him to think about things he didn't particularly care to explore. "You mean like you encouraged Sophie to be?"

"Yes," he replied simply. "Now, if you'll excuse me, I have a whole…" He pointed to a stack of grant requests.

Killian ignored that. "You know, love really requires trust of another sort."

Sawyer tried to keep working. "Trust is trust. Killian, I really have to—"

"Actually, it's not."

Sawyer tossed his pen on the desk, accepting that he wasn't going to avoid Killian's need to counsel.

"Love asks you to trust that the lover is going to respect your feelings, even when they don't make sense. In fact—and all the current books may disagree with me on this, but I still think it's the only thing that works—it may ask you sometimes to amend what you believe for the peace of mind of the lover, particularly if what the person wants of you isn't selfish or morally wrong, just…misguided. Like Sophie's wanting you to be safe."

Sawyer pretended surprise. "Really. I had no idea where you were going with this."

"Don't be smart. You've made the foundation far more productive than we ever imagined it could be when we developed the idea. You've done more for charities in this country than anyone, and you give yourself without condition to everyone in our family and to your friends." Killian came to lean his hands on the front of Sawyer's desk and smiled at him. Sawyer remembered that look from when they were children and his brother was trying to sway him to his way of thinking.

"However you believe you failed Abby when she was taken, you've more than made up for. You no longer have anything to prove to any of us. You've done it. But now you do have a few things to prove to Sophie. She has to know her feelings are safe with you, that you won't just dismiss them because you don't agree.'' He uttered a self-deprecating laugh. ''I learned that one the hard way. Stop the stunts, Sawyer.''

Killian was right. Sawyer had known that the minute the limo drove away with his future. He'd tried to bury the truth in work, but it kept surfacing, nagging at him. ''I have to do this one.''

Killian nodded. ''I realize that. But maybe if you explain that this is the final one, she'll come back to you.''

Sawyer thought that was a rosy view of the situation. ''Okay. Thanks. Now can I get some work done?''

Killian nodded, but he stood slowly, as though he had more on his mind. ''Campbell tell you he's leaving?''

''Yeah.''

''Doesn't sound like he's going to be talked out of it.''

''No. I guess we'll just have to trust that deep down he's aware that this is his home and he'll come back once in a while.''

''That's what I told him. He said you understood why he has to go.''

Sawyer smiled grimly. ''I don't, but everybody should feel there's someone out there who understands.''

Killian patted him on the shoulder. ''And that was the point of this whole conversation.

''What about the DNA test?'' Killian asked Sawyer while he walked to the door. ''Shouldn't we be getting the results pretty soon?''

Sawyer nodded. ''Any day. Mom's getting antsy.''

''Yeah. China just keeps smiling, but she seems to wander off by herself more often.''

''I like her. It'd be nice if it was her. See you at dinner.''

SOPHIE SPENT THE DAY refusing to think about Sawyer riding through the ring of fire that evening at the fairgrounds. As part of the hospital staff, helping host the event, she was assigned to sell raffle tickets, but she intended to hide in her car while Sawyer's stunt was taking place.

She'd put him out of her life, yet thoughts of him continued to occupy her mind, indeed her every waking moment, and that surprised her.

Molly, knowing Sophie would be busy tonight, volunteered to take all the children with her to the fairgrounds. ''That way you won't have to worry about anything but the booth. And if you should decide to find Sawyer before he goes flying into danger, and tell him you've been…oh, I don't know…*a twit, a goose, an idiot!*…then when he forgives you, you won't have to worry about what your kids are doing.''

Sophie had frowned at her friend. ''Molly, I know you mean well,'' she said, ''but your life and mine have been very different and you can't possibly understand what I need now.''

''All any woman needs is a wonderful man who loves her and her children. What else is there that can't be worked out?''

"What if he kills himself?" Sophie demanded, her eyes filling with tears, as they had every time she thought about the risk. "What good is this wonderful man going to do me and my children then?"

"Maybe if you tell him you love him and support him," Molly suggested, "he won't be worried that he's lost you and he'll be able to focus so that he *doesn't* kill himself. Did you ever think of that? He did promise that this would be his last wild stunt."

"How did you know that?" Sophie demanded.

"Gracie told Kayla."

Of course. Everyone was on Sawyer's side—her own children included.

In pale pink cotton capris and top, Sophie wound her hair into a knot, donned a pair of small silver hoop earrings with a pink bead in the middle of each hoop, then shouldered a big straw purse. She walked to her car and found the Abbotts' limousine pulling in beside it.

She put her purse on the hood of her car and went to speak to Daniel. "Hi, Daniel," she said. "What are you doing here?"

"We're here to pick you up for the fund-raiser," he replied.

"We?" she asked.

The side window in the back slid down and Chloe's pretty face peered out. "Get in, Sophie," she commanded. "I want to talk to you."

"Mrs. Abbott, there's nothing…" she began to protest. But Daniel had slipped out from behind the wheel, walked around the limo and opened the back door on the opposite side.

"Please, Mrs. Foster," he said.

With a defeated sigh, Sophie retrieved her purse from the hood of her car and climbed in opposite Chloe. Tante Bijou was seated beside her niece, dressed for the occasion in blue jeans and a long jeans jacket decorated with beads.

Chloe wore a white pantsuit with gold epaulets and buttons. Sophie wondered if the epaulets were responsible for her commanding manner.

"If Sawyer knew I was doing this," Chloe said with an apologetic smile, "he'd be very upset. But I feel obliged to try to explain him to you, anyway."

"You don't have to do that," Sophie insisted. "I know what a good person he is and how he does these stunts because they raise so much money for charity. I understand that his reasons are noble. I just can't live with the worry."

Chloe shook her head at her. "What about the worry of never finding another man like him?"

Sophie didn't want to be talked out of her feelings, and she didn't know how to answer that, anyway. The years ahead looked very bleak. She settled simply for, "At least I wouldn't have to always be afraid."

"Sophie." Chloe reached across the gap that separated them and put her hand on hers. "I've heard about how much you've suffered, and though that kind of thing is completely outside my experience, I can imagine what it was like. And I can imagine the wonderful freedom you must feel at not having to live like that anymore, but avoiding a relationship to avoid any and all fears, isn't the answer, either."

Sophie put her other hand on top of Chloe's. "I'm safe now. I don't want to deal with fear again."

"You think you can live without ever being afraid

again? You'd have to care about nothing. Are you going to keep your children safe their whole lives by locking them in their closets?''

On one level, Sophie knew she was right, but on another, she just couldn't let herself accept that.

"Sawyer takes these risks," Sophie accused quietly, "to prove something."

Sophie nodded and tightened her grip on her hand. "All the boys feel responsible for Abby's kidnapping. Killian was away, Sawyer slept through it right on the other side of her nursery door and Campbell had pushed her out of his room that day, when all she'd wanted was someone to play with. Such innocent, childish crimes turned into adult burdens because a life was taken from us."

Chloe's eyes filled with tears, and Sophie tried to stop her from going on. "Please, Mrs. Abbott—"

"No, you must listen. Sawyer started all this to prove himself fearless—you're absolutely right. But I think he's done it. He distributes our foundation money with insight and great generosity, he uses his position in this community and that fearlessness you so suspect to make money for yet more charities, and he's selfless with anyone who needs him. You've seen that in your own case, Kezia tells me."

"Yes," Sophie had to admit, remembering all the time he'd spent with her and her children, all his kindnesses to them, that night she'd worked late and he'd changed her whole future as a woman.

"Sharing a life with him will require a fearless woman," Chloe went on. "You're no longer in an abusive relationship, so fear is something you impose upon yourself. Life gives and takes with both hands, and if you're going to accept life's gifts, you have to be willing to relinquish them. And then live for all you have right now.''

Daniel pulled into the fairgrounds parking lot, and Sophie simply sat there while he helped Chloe out of the limo, got a wheelchair out of the back for Tante Bijou, then lifted her out and into it.

Fear is something you impose upon yourself. She thought over Chloe's words, wondering why that had never occurred to her. Probably, she considered wryly, because she'd never been in a situation before where fear was a choice—Bill had filled her with fear. But he was gone and her life now was fresh and new. Maybe…she didn't have to be afraid. Maybe she could just trust Sawyer to know what he was doing. Maybe she could believe that her feelings for him were so strong they would keep him safe. And that life with him, even with the stunts, was better than life without him.

She felt an emotional knot release at that thought, as though she'd freed herself of the last grip of her past.

Daniel offered her a hand out of the limo and she hugged Chloe.

"Thank you," she said. "I do love him very much. And the possibility of not having him forever…"

"I know," Chloe said. "But if you love each other as fearlessly as you can, then there will never be regrets, whatever happens."

"I have to find him," Sophie said, looking out over the large crowd of people already wandering among the booths.

"Yes, you do," she said.

The evening was beginning to shadow, the lights growing brighter as Sophie covered every inch of the fairgrounds. The perfumed air mingled with the homey smells of kettle corn, cotton candy, hot dogs and the baked goods at the church ladies' booth.

She ran into everyone but Sawyer. She found Killian and Cordie walking hand in hand, Brian and China firing air rifles at wooden geese, Molly with all the children at the ice-cream booth.

Sophie offered each of the children another five dollars.

"You already gave us spending money, Mom," Gracie reminded her. "What's going on?"

"Nothing." She didn't want to tell her she was feeling lighthearted because she finally understood that fear had become such a habit she'd forgotten she could make it a choice. She didn't want to tell her she was looking for Sawyer, because if she found him and he still didn't understand or was unwilling to believe that she was sorry, nothing would change, anyway. "I just want you to have fun. Try all the rides and eat whatever you want."

Now Gracie *was* worried. "Eat whatever we want? Mom, are you okay?"

Sophie hugged her, then Emma and Eddie and Kayla and Molly. "I'm fine. You all have a good time and I'll find you later."

She located the hospital's booth just as Jack was checking his watch. She'd been due to take over for him ten minutes ago.

"Have you seen Sawyer?" she asked anxiously.

"He's not coming until just before the stunt," he replied, studying her warily. As Molly's husband and

Kayla's father, he was also privy to all her personal business. "I heard about what happened. You're not thinking of yelling at him or—?"

"Jack, for heaven's sake."

"Well, I just want to be sure. He's been upset, too. He's at Lou Bergman's. They're inspecting the bike one more time to make sure everything's in good shape."

"How does he seem today?" she asked worriedly.

"He's always in control, but I'm sure you're on his mind. You ready to take over here?"

"Sure," she agreed, her heart sinking. She wanted to see Sawyer before the stunt. She wanted to tell him she loved him. She didn't want him to be upset when he was flying through fire.

"Can I slip away to watch the stunt?" she asked.

He seemed surprised. "I thought that the way you felt, you wouldn't want to."

"I don't," she admitted candidly, "but I feel I should. Maybe I can will him to be safe."

He patted her shoulder. "Of course you can. Everybody will be watching it, anyway. There won't be anyone to sell tickets to."

"Thanks, Jack."

He handed her a package of cookies with the church ladies sticker on it. "Here's something to keep you going for a while."

"Thank you." She stashed the cookies under the booth's counter, unable to think of food for the moment.

Business at the booth was brisk. The one-week trip to the Virgin Islands with airfare and accommodations attracted many people, so that Sophie was forced to concentrate on making change and worried only between spurts of customers.

Fear and worry, she told herself, were not the same thing.

She watched the crowd when she could, looking for familiar features, hoping Sawyer would change his mind about arriving just for the stunt and might even come in search of her. His spiked blond hair would be visible even in the lantern-lit darkness. But there was no sign of him.

Everyone in his family eventually appeared at the booth to buy tickets. She asked Campbell if he'd seen Sawyer and got the same answer Jack had given her. Kezia and Daniel walked by holding hands. Chloe appeared with Winfield, who was pushing Tante Bijou in the wheelchair so that she could negotiate the fair in comfort. Tante Bijou bought one hundred tickets, telling Sophie a long story in French, her eyes sparkling.

Chloe smiled and patted her aunt's shoulder. "She says she met her third husband in the Virgin Islands. And he was the most fun of all of them."

Their conversation was interrupted by a voice on a loudspeaker, inviting everyone to gather at the far end of the field, where the motorcycle stunt was about to take place.

Sophie's heart lurched against her ribs.

"Mon Dieu!" Chloe exclaimed quietly, less secure than her pep talk to Sophie had suggested she was.

Sophie closed the booth, stuffed the money into her purse for safekeeping and followed Sawyer's family to the field. Killian waved them to join Cordie and him at a spot where they could all stand together. China, Brian and Campbell were already there.

Molly brought Gracie, Eddie and Emma to her. "Jack has to introduce Sawyer," she said, "and I have to make sure there's no ice cream on his tie or lettuce in his teeth. Can Kayla stay with you?"

"Of course."

Sophie barely had a voice, but when Gracie eyed her questioningly, she simply smiled and led the girls to join the family. Killian lifted Emma so that she could see, and Campbell put Eddie on his shoulders. Sophie stood between the girls, needing their support.

The high-school band played a number, then Jack took the small stage to the side of the field and announced that the evening had already netted a small fortune—and they still had a few more hours to go.

Sophie wanted to listen, but all she could focus on were the takeoff and landing ramps sitting on the field, and the pole to which a large metal circle probably four or five feet across was attached. The four firemen in full gear who stood nearby, armed with fire retardant, belied the innocuousness of the apparatuses.

Sophie made herself look away.

"Thanks to the daring of one of Losthampton's favorite citizens, Sawyer Abbott," he said, "the hospital's new equipment is a done deal."

The crowd applauded, and Sawyer's brothers whistled and cheered.

And then Sawyer stepped onstage. He was dressed in a silver suit decorated with yellow-and-orange flames, and held a matching helmet under his arm. He waved at the audience, quickly blew a kiss toward his family. Sophie was sure he hadn't spotted her in the audience.

"Thank you for supporting this cause," he said with a broad smile. He was the picture of confidence and competence, she thought. No suggestion of a broken heart, no evidence that he missed her.

And quite possibly, he didn't. He'd led an exciting, fun-filled life before her children had thrust her into it, and he was probably relieved to be back in it, back with the lively women who occupied it, rather than having to second-guess his every move with her.

"Our hospital is filled with brilliant and dedicated people," he said, then added with an artlessly modest hand to his chest, "who've patched me up so many times I *have* to support them. So, here I go."

Laughter rippled through the crowd as he waved again and loped off the stage toward the shiny black motorcycle, also painted with flames.

Sophie's heart pounded so hard she couldn't hear what Jack was saying.

SAWYER CLIMBED ASTRIDE the bike and put on his helmet as Jack thanked Lou Bergman for the loan of the motorcycle and the ramps, and Seaboard Circus for providing the fire ring.

He tried to focus, but it was hard. He'd thought he'd seen Eddie on somebody's shoulders in the group at the end of the field, where Killian had told him the family would be. Did that mean Sophie was here? That part of the field was out of his vision now, and he wished he were confident enough in her love for him that he could feel her presence.

But he couldn't. He just felt as he had since their

argument—lonely and depressed. Giving away the foundation's money had helped a little, but his life was about even more than the Abbott Mills philanthropy now. Or, it had been.

The band began to play again; that meant it was almost time for the stunt. He had to get himself together or he would be charred Abbott. He tried to remember Killian's comment. Love trusted that the lover understood.

He closed his eyes and thought about Sophie, concentrated on how much he'd enjoyed her company, how remarkable making love with her had been—how much he wanted that for the rest of his life.

Then the band began the drumroll.

He walked the bike into position, tested that his helmet was secure and revved the motor. Everything felt right.

He rode in a circle, then he did it again, waiting for that oneness-with-the-bike feeling that meant he was ready. And there it was, the thrumming of the motor that became the thrumming of his blood. He picked up speed and headed for the ramp.

The ring ignited and a communal gasp rose from the audience, loud enough for Sawyer to hear it through his helmet. He tuned it out. The stunt would take only seconds and he couldn't split his concentration.

He raced toward the fire. The color was gruesomely beautiful. He could feel the heat, see the flames reaching for him.

He felt the bike leave the ramp, sail right into the heart of the fire—and out of the flame. In the crowd speeding by, he saw Sophie's face smiling...

Smiling?

He almost lost it. He leaned forward to maintain the forward thrust of his body, wondering if he'd actually seen that or had simply wanted it. Willing the bike through the air, he landed with bone-jarring finality on the other side. He even managed to keep his seat.

The cheers roared in his ears. He pulled off his helmet and wiped the sweat from his eyes, to see his family running toward him—God!—Sophie in the lead.

SOPHIE WAS HAPPY to risk rejection as she ran toward him. Her heart wasn't working, anyway. It hadn't felt anything since it had stalled when she'd watched the bike seem to stop in the middle of the flames, as though it might drop right there.

She'd reached for him with her love and pulled him through.

He tossed his helmet and caught her in both arms, lifting her high against him, crushing her to him.

"Sophie!" he laughed. "You came!"

"I did," she replied, kissing him over and over. "I love you so much. I'm sorry I was selfish."

"You weren't selfish," he corrected her. "You were right. I have to think about it differently now. This was it. We'll find other way to help raise money."

Her children threw themselves at him, then his family hugged him one by one. China held back, waiting for her turn.

Sophie hugged her. "I can't tell you how glad I am that's over!"

"I know. I think we all are. I'm a basket case."

"I'll bet you'll be relieved when the DNA results arrive."

China hitched a shoulder in a small gesture of embarrassment, then indicated a white envelope protruding from the front pocket of her purse. "It arrived by courier this afternoon while everyone else was getting ready for tonight."

"And?"

"I didn't open it. I want to do it with Chloe," she said, "but I didn't want her to be worried about anything but Sawyer tonight."

Sophie could only imagine what that had cost the young woman.

Then someone caught China's arm and she was drawn into Sawyer's embrace.

"Congratulations!" China exclaimed. "It's a real gift to flirt with fire and never get burned."

He drew Sophie into his other arm. "Yeah, well, my flirting days are over." He kissed Sophie soundly. "I need something cold to drink. Let's go see if we can drain the pop stand dry."

The pop stand, operated by the Kiwanis Club, served soft drinks, juice and bottled water. They had borrowed several pavilions from the town's Sunday market and placed picnic tables under them. With twinkle lights strung from corner to corner, the effect was surprisingly intimate.

All the Abbotts crowded inside, the ladies sitting, the men standing, Eddie and Emma chasing each other around the perimeter. Gracie and Kayla stood just outside, watching a group of boys wrestling over a soccer ball. One moment they rolled their eyes over the juvenile antics, but when the boys looked their way, they giggled.

Sophie smiled over that very typical response. Her daughter was going to be all right. Learning the truth about her father had traumatized Gracie, but she was smart and she would find a balance between fear and trust—just as her mother finally had.

Sawyer had pulled off his fire suit and now he put a jeans-clad knee on the bench beside her and leaned over her to kiss her. "I saw you," he said softly while the family talked and laughed, "when I was right in the middle of the flames. But I couldn't believe it. I almost made the bike stall."

"I noticed that," she said, smiling into his love-filled eyes with her heart in hers. "I kept telling you I loved you, hoping that would pull you out the other side of the ring."

His gaze roved her face, then settled on her eyes again with happiness. "It did."

"You did that for me," she whispered. "Brought me through the fire. I love you for that. And for a million other reasons."

"Well, you have to explain each and every one of them to me tonight," he said, kissing her gently. "Then I'll list all the reasons I love you."

Chloe's little scream of surprise startled them out of their erotic promises. They looked up, to find the family staring at her. She sat across the table from Sophie between Cordie and China, who sat on the end. She held China's hand up. It held the couriered letter from the DNA lab.

"The results are here!" Chloe said. "Open it!"

China hesitated, as though suddenly afraid. Then

she swallowed and slid a fingernail under the flap of the envelope.

"Wait!" Killian said. "Whatever that contains, we're all agreed she stays on as estate manager, right?" He looked around for confirmation. "With Campbell leaving, we're going to need her more than ever."

Everyone nodded.

Nervously, China pulled the folded sheet of paper out of the envelope. She closed her eyes for a moment, then opened them and perused the letter. For a moment, it was impossible to tell what she'd read. Then she put a hand over her mouth and handed Chloe the letter.

She slipped off the bench, turned back toward all the waiting, anxious faces and said tearfully, "I'm not your sister."

Then she appeared to look desperately for somewhere to run. Despite the hostilities that had prevailed between them, Campbell opened his arms to her and she went into them. He tucked her close and walked her away toward the woods.

Chloe burst into tears and Killian went to put his arms around her. "It's all right, Mom," he said, his own voice thick. "We'll just...adopt her."

Chloe nodded, but her heart was broken. Sophie stood to wrap her arms around Sawyer. "I'm sorry," she said.

He held her tightly. "Yeah, me, too." His voice was uneven. "I wanted her to be Abby."

After a moment, Chloe sniffed, took a sip of her bottled water and assumed the matriarchal demeanor that meant she had something to say.

"Well. That isn't the news we wanted," she said. "But even if she isn't Abby, it doesn't mean we can't love her like a daughter and a sister, anyway. Love has brought us Cordie and Sophie and the children, and it's about to bring us two new babies. So I think we should just believe that Abbott love will bring Abigail back to us one day."

Sawyer reached for his pop cup. "We should toast to that."

He pulled Gracie, Eddie, Emma and Kayla in to join the toast. "To Abbott love," he said.

They raised glasses, cups and bottles, and the toast rang across the field. "To Abbott love!"

Then Sawyer turned to Sophie, raised his glass again and whispered, "To my love for you."

She clinked her cup against his, her heart overflowing. "To mine for you."

HARLEQUIN®

AMERICAN *Romance*®

TIMES TWO

Heartwarming stories with truly twinspirational characters!

THE MIRACLE TWINS
by Lisa Bingham

Harlequin American Romance #1032

Foreign correspondent Lucy Devon never pictured herself with kids, but when she comes across orphaned twin girls who need her help, she can't say no. More to the point, the babies need medical help—the kind only Dr. Nick Hammond, Lucy's ex-fiancé, can provide. Suddenly, Lucy finds herself dreaming of motherhood—and of Nick. But there was a reason she'd broken up with Nick on the day of their wedding…wasn't there?

Available August 2004
wherever Harlequin books are sold.

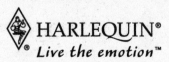

HARLEQUIN®
® *Live the emotion*™

www.americanromances.com

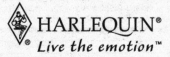

If you enjoyed what you just read,
then we've got an offer you can't resist!

Take 2 bestselling
love stories FREE!
Plus get a FREE surprise gift!

Clip this page and mail it to Harlequin Reader Service®

IN U.S.A.	IN CANADA
3010 Walden Ave.	P.O. Box 609
P.O. Box 1867	Fort Erie, Ontario
Buffalo, N.Y. 14240-1867	L2A 5X3

YES! Please send me 2 free Harlequin American Romance® novels and my free surprise gift. After receiving them, if I don't wish to receive anymore, I can return the shipping statement marked cancel. If I don't cancel, I will receive 4 brand-new novels every month, before they're available in stores! In the U.S.A., bill me at the bargain price of $4.24 plus 25¢ shipping & handling per book and applicable sales tax, if any*. In Canada, bill me at the bargain price of $4.99 plus 25¢ shipping & handling per book and applicable taxes**. That's the complete price and a savings of at least 10% off the cover prices—what a great deal! I understand that accepting the 2 free books and gift places me under no obligation ever to buy any books. I can always return a shipment and cancel at any time. Even if I never buy another book from Harlequin, the 2 free books and gift are mine to keep forever.

154 HDN DZ7S
354 HDN DZ7T

Name	(PLEASE PRINT)	
Address	Apt.#	
City	State/Prov.	Zip/Postal Code

* Terms and prices subject to change without notice. Sales tax applicable in N.Y.
** Canadian residents will be charged applicable provincial taxes and GST.
  All orders subject to approval. Offer limited to one per household and not valid to
  current Harlequin American Romance® subscribers.
  ® are registered trademarks owned and used by the trademark owner and or its licensee.

AMER04   ©2004 Harlequin Enterprises Limited

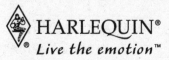

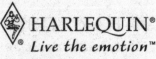